ABOUT THE AUTHOR

RJ Scott lives in the Chiltern hills just outside London. She loves reading anything from thrillers to sci-fi to horror; however, her first real love will always be the world of romance. Her goal is to write stories with a heart of romance, a troubled road to reach happiness, and more than a hint of happily ever after.

Email:
rj@rjscott.co.uk

Webpage:
www.rjscott.co.uk

Facebook:
http://www.facebook.com/rjscotts

Twitter:
@rjscotts

ALL THE KING'S

RJ SCOTT

SILVERPUBLISHING
Published by Silver Publishing
Publisher of Erotic Romance

If you purchased this book without a cover you should be aware that this book is stolen property. It was reported as "unsold and destroyed" to the publisher, and neither the author nor the publisher has received any payment for this "stripped book."

SILVER PUBLISHING

ISBN 978-1-61495-322-7

All The King's Men

Copyright © 2011 by RJ Scott
Editor: Devin Govaere
Cover Artist: Reese Dante

All rights reserved. Except for use in any review, the reproduction or utilization of this work in whole or in part in any form by any electronic, mechanical or other means, now known or hereafter invented, including xerography, photocopying and recording, or in any information storage or retrieval system, is forbidden without the written permission of the editorial office, Silver Publishing, 18530 Mack Avenue, Box 253, Grosse Pointe Farms, MI 48236, USA.

All characters in this book have no existence outside the imagination of the author and have no relation whatsoever to anyone bearing the same name or names. They are not even distantly inspired by any individual known or unknown to the author, and all incidents are pure invention.

Visit Silver Publishing at https://spsilverpublishing.com

DEDICATION

For Devin, who really walked through fire for this one.
And for Invisible Mark $^{(TM)}$, the greatest important non-character ever in literature…

For Reese
I promise to go with first instinct all the time…

For Gayle and Chris Quinton… for all your help with this and for your friendship which always makes me smile.
peng

And *always* for my family

TRADEMARKS ACKNOWLEDGEMENT

The author acknowledges the trademarked status and trademark owners of the following wordmarks mentioned in this work of fiction:

iPhone: Apple, Inc.
Nike: Nike, Inc.
Wal-Mart: Wal-Mart Stores, Inc.
Google: Google, Inc.
Band-aid: Johnson & Johnson

Humpty Dumpty sat on a wall,
Humpty Dumpty had a great fall.
All the king's horses and all the king's men
Couldn't put Humpty together again!

PROLOGUE

California is one of America's most earthquake-prone states.

The boundary between the massive Pacific and North American tectonic plates, the notorious San Andreas Fault, runs roughly southeast to northwest through much of California. In addition, a jumble of lesser transverse faults clutters the map of the state.

Both sides of the San Andreas Fault move in a northwest direction, but at different speeds, causing geologic tension to build. That tension is released in the form of an earthquake. The possibility is always present for associated earthquakes among the nearby transform faults.

The U.S. Geological Survey says the state faces a forty-six percent chance of being hit by a Richter Scale magnitude 7.5 or higher earthquake in the next thirty years.

Possibly even next year.

CHAPTER 1

Thursday 6:52 a.m.

"Tell me you aren't considering going to see him."

Nathan Richardson hesitated, shifting the phone from one hand to the other, aware that Jason was waiting for an answer, glad his friend wasn't actually standing here to see the guilt on his face. Leaning against the gate to the park, he took in a deep breath of fresh air. Not for the first time when his ex was being discussed, he wished he knew what to say. Jason was his closest friend since moving to LA, and fuelled by alcohol and pizza, Jason had listened to Nathan talk about the whole Ryan/Nathan breakup at length. None of that mattered, because however much they talked, Jason would never be able to understand how much Ryan had shaped Nathan's life, how much he'd meant to him.

He'd last seen Jason three days ago at a script read through, and then after when they shared tequila and talk back at Jason's apartment in downtown LA. Jason had listened to Nathan's confused explanations of why he didn't love Ryan and why he couldn't love Ryan. Jason had listened patiently, and then pointed out very succinctly that, Nathan loved Ryan "the asshole."

Nathan had argued himself blue that he and Ryan were over, finished. Halting sentences filled with conviction in a way that was a direct result of alcohol. It was the morning after that rambling conversation that Nathan had finally admitted to himself what Jason could see as the truth. He still loved Ryan, and he needed to stop loving Ryan if he wanted to save his sanity.

"I need to talk to him, Jason."

"By all accounts, many of them from your own mouth, he is a manipulative, jealous, possessive, lying, untrusting asshole." Jason was working up a head of steam, and as usual, Nathan's first response to that was defense against the relationship that had meant so much to him.

"Jase —I told you— it wasn't all him. We were a long way apart, and it was my idea to—"

"Don't. Seriously. Just don't start with all that *I moved to LA so it's my fault* crap."

"I still love him, I think I always will," Nathan finally offered sadly. He knew the accusations were now going to fly. Jason had become Nathan's friend in LA through the soap they both acted on, and they were as close as two men in the business could be without actually being in a sexual relationship with each other. The two bright lights in his life, Ryan his ex-lover and Jason his friend, had only met once. The night Nathan's relationship with

Ryan had self-destructed. Jason had left in a hurry that night when Nathan asked him to go. But he'd heard stories from Nathan when Nathan was at his lowest since the breakup and, more importantly, under the influence of copious amounts of alcohol.

"He screwed around on you, Nate, or do I have to remind you of the het sex with that brunette?"

"Allison? Hell, you don't need to remind me," Nathan replied tiredly. That one fact, clearly made worse because Ryan had chosen a woman as a weapon of vengeance, was what his friend used to remind him at every possible occasion. He wiped sweat from his forehead, pushing his hair back from his face and stretching out the tightened muscles from his daily workout to stay healthy. Keeping fit hurt. Still, it was one way of forgetting his ex-lover in his down time, when he actually had days off. It helped him to forget intense brown eyes and dark hair and a smile that could slay him at ten paces.

"Just be careful— yeah? Don't go calling him with guilt and shit. Think about the person you are here in LA, the confident, happy, successful actor. Swear to me that, if you're gonna call him, you call me first and we talk."

"Jason—"

"Swear it, Nate."

"I promise. I'll think of what I want to say and I will

run it by you first." Jason made a noise of agreement, and they exchanged goodbyes.

Nathan pocketed his cell and leaned against the park gates, brooding and wondering exactly what his next move needed to be. His gaze passed over where he now lived, a place so very different from his and Ryan's former home in the chaos and noise of New York.

A small complex of four apartments, quiet and remote, the peace and solitude suited his frame of mind perfectly. He lived in this two bedroom apartment in the hills beyond LA, rented from an absentee landlord and had made his own with photos of family and his modeling portfolio. He was standing in the rough-hewn park carved out across the road from his home, and he looked back away from his sanctuary to the nature that surrounded him. The park itself was a jumble of trees and rocks, grass and pathways, some steeply climbing higher into the hills, some gently curving and ideal for his attempted runs. The nearest main road was a quarter mile away, and most people drove past the entrance to the small complex without realizing the road led to people's homes.

He smiled as a cloud of birds rose gracefully from the oak at the edge of the park, heading skyward at an incredible speed. He loved that he was so close to the peace of nature, and the sight of the birds was both eerie and fascinating. He couldn't stop looking at it, wishing he had his camera with him, cursing at another amazing photo opportunity lost.

He couldn't wait to share what he'd seen with Ryan.

Nathan stifled his instinctive response. Why the hell couldn't he process a new train of thought that didn't include that name? The thought of his ex-lover made him fear his heart breaking there and then…again.

* * * *

Thursday 6:59 am

"What brings you to LA?"

"Work." *Nathan.*

The taxi driver ferrying Ryan Ortiz into the hills peppered him with the usual questions.

"So you're not a resident?"

"No, I'm here from New York, just for a few days."

The questions continued to come. What did he think of the spate of forest fires in the LA hills? Did he think that Lindsay Lohan was for real? Did he have pets? Was he married? For the most part, Ryan managed to keep up until he realized that the driver wasn't actually listening to his answers; and so he was able to subside to a new level of tired grunts in answer to each new question. Still dazed from his early morning flight from Phoenix, his mind limped through thought and memory, attempting to make order out of chaos. The views from the taxi, the vista of the city laid out through the misty smog, were gorgeous, and he itched for his camera. It was a very strange feeling not to have it with him, but the rush to get here, to see Nathan, had precluded organizing his extensive camera equipment. It was the first time in his memory he'd gone anywhere without at least one camera.

Ryan's passion for photography had led him to meet Nathan.

Ryan had landed the job as lead photographer for *Mode Style*, the magazine the fashion industry liked to call their bible. The masses simply nicknamed the glossy mag *Style*. His arrival had been heralded with great fanfare. At twenty-five, he was the youngest member of the photographic team, with an excellent portfolio covering six years of experience at other publications.

During the interview, he'd been asked why he didn't freelance. Ryan wanted security, something that had been severely lacking in his younger life. However, the interviewer didn't need to be told that. Accordingly, he answered her question as honestly as he could without undue personal revelations, simply saying he wanted the stability to grow as a photographer— to become better.

Style was the cutting edge. Ryan wanted to develop his skills and to advance *Style*'s image. His second reason for pursuing the position was the opportunity to work in New York City, not to mention there were benefits, healthcare, and a slew of gorgeous models and their agents fighting for ad space.

Most importantly to Ryan, though, was the fact that New York City was his spiritual home. Orphaned at three, he had entered the "system" and had been moved, for one reason or another, from foster home to foster home. When he was moved for the last time, however, his newest set of foster parents, Mr and Mrs Ortiz, bought him a second-hand camera and he found his reason for being: photography. Photography became his way of expressing himself, and when he started to sell some of his photos, it was even a way of supporting himself financially.

Nathan had been the model for Ryan's first shoot for *Style*. It had been a high-end fashion shoot, which, ironically, needed the teen model more out of clothes than in. He'd been so beautiful, even then, only nineteen, fresh from a midsize horse farm in Kentucky, with blond silky hair, pouty lips, and eyes that promised sin. It was incredibly difficult for Ryan to keep it in his pants that first time. Nathan, with his high cheekbones and his startling green eyes, was enough to tempt a saint. Still, twenty-five-year-old Ryan was *so* not going there, not that week anyway.

When Nathan turned twenty-one, Ryan made a move. They were near the end of another shoot for *Style*, just the two of them. They'd spent hours catching Nathan in all the different lights of day, repeating poses and not-poses until he'd been relaxed enough to let his body lead him. Catching the change in Nathan's reactions, Ryan had shot endlessly, cueing until his voice had gone raspy. Then letting Nathan cue himself.

It was *the* shoot, the one that Ryan knew would push Nathan up and away from *Style*. Nathan had taken the session and made it his own, owning the scenes and transforming them just by his presence. Nathan had shown a glimmer of what he was capable of doing, and Ryan felt like he'd discovered gold. Maybe it was the presence of Nathan's ever more apparent maturity, or possibly even the realization that he was watching Nathan step from adolescence to adulthood. Whatever it was, something made him put his hands on Nathan's shoulders and invite the younger man to his apartment. Ryan didn't remember making a conscious decision to do that: the words just fell out of his mouth in a tumble of lust and want. Nathan said *no*, his green eyes serious.

"I don't do that," he said simply, pulling back out of Ryan's gentle hold.

"Do what?"

"I don't go back to photographers' apartments for sex." Nathan was firm, no nonsense, his expression determined.

For a moment, Ryan was confused, then he realized Nathan had clearly meant he didn't do casual sex. Ryan hadn't been that implicit in his proposal, and he wished he could take back his careless words.

Nathan stuck his arms through the sleeves of his white shirt and yanked it down, covering the beauty of young, hairless, warm-toned skin previously on display.

"That's not…I don't want…sex."

Well, he sounded like an idiot but he'd at least attempted to defend himself. Then he'd had blown it big time. "You are gay though, right?"

Ryan cringed at that memory: what a crass, stupid, pointless thing to say. He'd given the impression that he thought the label *gay* equaled an automatic need for casual sex and easy lays. Nathan had been courteous. He obviously hadn't wanted to be rude to the photographer who could literally make or break his modeling career.

"Yes, gay, but no, I don't want to go back to your apartment with you."

What could he possibly say to defend how he'd just come across? He'd sounded like some 1940's director with a casting couch.

"I'm not expecting sex for photos," he'd blurted out, to which Nathan had simply raised an eyebrow.

Grabbing his duffle, Nathan had left with a few words thrown over his shoulder. "Whatever you say."

Of course, after analyzing the whole thing, Ryan had finally acted on his attraction after a shoot for underwear. After what seemed to be years, but was only a few months, he had Nathan exactly where he wanted him—naked and pleading, pinned under him, writhing as his orgasm hit him, words of desperate need spilling from his mouth.

It was a one night stand: that was all, just for Ryan to scratch the itch. Then it became a short term thing they enjoyed between shoots. Then Nathan moved in. Ryan bought his young lover a platinum ring and promised him the rest of his natural life. It had been so easy. Their relationship had withstood so much that had been thrown at it, not the least of which was the ugliness and bitchiness of the circles they moved in. Nathan was vocally in love, and Ryan was content with what they had.

Then Hollywood happened. Nathan had always wanted to try acting. Based on the quality of his acting skills, he'd won a small part in a sprawling night-time soap opera. Suddenly Nathan was in LA and Ryan was in New York. At first they were sure they could handle the situation. They met as often as they could and talked every night on the phone. They vowed it was good for their relationship to have some time apart and that everything was going to be all right. Until abruptly, finally, and utterly irreversibly, it wasn't.

One week, after a particularly hard editorial meeting, Ryan was exhausted, bitchy, and missed Nathan something awful. A last minute cancellation in his calendar meant he could fly to LA. When he arrived at Nathan's apartment in the hills, it was to find Nathan entertaining a fellow actor from the show, a guy called Jason, someone far too friendly to be sitting on the sofa with *his* Nathan.

Nathan had sworn there was nothing to it. It turned out, after the fact, that actually there hadn't been anything to it. Nevertheless, the incident and their heated words had been enough to send Ryan a few weeks before Christmas, bitter and resentful and stinging with embarrassment at his misassumptions, to the arms of an ex, a model from one of his shoots—Allison.

Love was love as far as he was concerned; gender had never been an issue for Ryan. He wasn't choosy, and didn't really label himself as bi. He just thought that getting off was just that. Self pity made him want to hurt Nathan and going to Allison was one big-assed way to achieve that.

Instant regret meant nothing when he admitted what he'd done. He threw himself at Nathan and begged for forgiveness, but it was over. Nathan wouldn't give him a second chance. Nathan left his position with *Style* and moved permanently to LA, embracing his burgeoning acting career and jettisoning Ryan from his life. Ryan was left with nothing, because of his own stupidity.

Then the spread in *Teen TV* magazine appeared, and it triggered a huge last chain reaction.

Nathan was being touted for a role in a TV series, up and away from his soap opera start. His picture was emblazoned on page twenty-nine opposite the article that discussed the information. The photo was one of Ryan's, and it was one of his favorites. Nathan, beautiful, shirtless, his lean body stretched with catlike grace, leaning back on his elbows. He gazed away from the camera, thoughtfully, his soft blond hair in disarray around his face. The photo was simply perfect.

Ryan had done it again. He'd run to Allison's new home in Phoenix, desperate for something, anything, to mend his heart, to rid himself of the ghost of Nathan Richardson. She gave him nothing other than a shoulder to cry on, happily sharing space with a new boyfriend who, from the way he hovered, clearly meant much more to her life than he ever had.

Ryan felt genuinely happy for her, and, for once, listened to what she said, and, surprisingly, agreed with everything. On her firm, no-nonsense instructions, he'd caught the first flight he possibly could to LA. Now he sat in the taxi as the driver steered it up into the hills. Allison had been right. He needed to push aside his insecurities, drop to his knees, and beg forgiveness of the one person who made him whole. She said it wouldn't be too late; he only hoped it wasn't.

* * * *

7:12 a.m.

After his pathetic half-hearted stumble run, Nathan decided he needed to get some more water and then, with the impetus to phone Ryan clear in his head, he went indoors at exactly 7:12 a.m. Despite Jason's words of caution, Nathan really wanted to see if maybe his ex-lover would agree to meet up, talk, find some kind of resolution. He was just inside the main door when the floor beneath his feet moved, subtly the first time, slowly, strongly, a groaning, a creaking, and a soft shaking. The strong, certain ground shift left him holding the doorframe. It only lasted a few seconds and was over before he could force a thought about it through the rest of the clutter in his mind. The checklist in his head clicked in automatically before the shaking had stopped. He smiled briefly. That earth movement would be dominating the news today. Hey, maybe today was a good day for him to walk proudly out of the closet! Surely revealing his sexual preferences would never be more newsworthy than an earthquake in Tinseltown.

He thumbed to the number of his brother out of state, and hit "Send". The phone at the other end rang once, twice, a third time, and voicemail kicked in. He decided not to leave a message. No one really needed to know that a minor shock had hit his apartment in the hills above LA. The trembler hadn't been strong enough to be worthy of hitting the national news anywhere outside of California. Nathan had just been trying to be a good citizen, letting a family member know, like the government said he should. He made a mental note to charge the damn cell when he had finished his shower.

Seconds later, just as Nathan pocketed his iPhone, the earth around him ripped apart with such savagery that it was impossible to stand upright. Nathan scrabbled to hold the side of the doorframe, trying to find his feet. His vision blurred as dust and concrete fell about his head, knocking him to the ground. Before the shaking stopped, before the ceiling joists cascaded down and trapped his legs, he slammed into unconsciousness.

CHAPTER 2

They were about ten minutes away from Nathan's apartment, ten minutes from possible relationship suicide, when the pre-shock hit. The driver cursed as the car skittered sideways, and Ryan grabbed on to the door and his belt in confusion.

"What the hell?"

"S'okay, just a small one. We get them all the time out here."

Ryan knew what he meant. Earthquake. He'd never really experienced an earthquake before and that had felt weird, like the whole of the earth beneath the car had slid sideways, stones and loose gravel from the hills above them dropping onto the car in a crashing, rattling rain.

Ryan peered out of the window; down at the sweeping vista of LA sleeping below him, wondering how many people woke up to the sound that was like distant thunder and to the shaking of the earth. The car had slewed to the edge of the road, and he shot a quick glance down the slope, thanking God that it hadn't been a major quake. Smiling ruefully, he sat back in the seat as the driver pulled away and angled back onto his side of the road.

A breath-stealing jolt yanked him from his musings.

The car was moving: no, the hill shuddered and fell,

pushing the hapless car ahead of it. The rocks, vegetation, the *sky* tumbled. The car neared the edge, the driver shouting hysterically as it tilted sideways, large chunks of hillside falling to dent the car, beat at the car, push the car, to the edge, to the drop, to the shaking and dancing of the moving earth.

Ryan clung with both hands to the grab handle over the cab's door and jerked at every noise, every motion. This wasn't good; not good at all. He stared out, snatching a quick look down at LA, and what he saw burned into his mind. Explosions. He thought he saw buildings shattering and imploding, but that had to be his imagination. *What the fuck is happening?*

The car ceased its crazy ride and, for one second, poised on the edge, overhanging the drop. Then a final shove of still moving dirt sent it careening, tumbling down the rise.

The car lodged against a natural outcrop and came to a sudden and bone-crunching stop, the thunder and passion of the earthquake still warring around it, the hill subsiding, plummeting and falling in a haphazard storm of rocks and debris. The seatbelt saved Ryan's life. It stopped him from being thrown from the car and crushed under it as it rolled and slid: but it also ultimately trapped him inside the vehicle as the chassis twisted and buckled against the onslaught of the hillside. All too soon the noises around him started to slow, and he was left in the dark, surrounded by dust and earth, his eyes burning with fumes. He needed to get out of the taxi *now*!

With a powerful resolution born of a desire to live, he heaved himself out of the belt and pushed at the door with his booted feet, tumbling out as it burst open. He crab-walked away from the compacted car, his eyes taking in what was essentially half a car. The front had been flattened, and the driver crushed.

He seemed trapped in a nightmare. The remains of the cab perched precariously on a bed of dirt and rocks of all sizes. Flames licked up leaking fuel, eating at the crushed metal. Ryan knew he could do nothing for the driver. He was gone…crushed…dead…*fuck*.

Stumbling to his feet, he clutched at his forehead, pulling his hand away and staring in a shocked stupor at the blood. A head injury. *Crap.*

The car groaned as the metal heated. Half out of his mind with horror and dread, believing the car would explode, he twisted and scrambled his way up over the remains of the road, feeling the heat on his back as the fire continued to eat away at the mutilated car. The cab wasn't the only car destroyed. One that had been ahead of them lay crushed so badly no one would have escaped. Another vehicle that they'd passed on the freeway had plowed into an embankment and burst into flames. All of them had been tossed around like toys in the hands of Nature.

Finally he crashed to his knees, his back to the view below. There was nothing he could do for anyone in any vehicle here, and his gaze focused on what was left of the road. Reluctantly, spurred by horrified fascination and the need to face what had happened, Ryan pushed himself to his feet and turned slowly. Shielding his eyes with his hand and coughing, he faced the nightmare vista of LA laid out before him. Fire. He could see fire, drifts of dark gray smoke, and clouds of dust. Debris. The ground still stirred uneasily beneath his feet. This was a living disaster movie, surreal, unbelievable. LA was unrecognizable. Everything had gone eerily silent where he stood above the rage of the distant fires and destruction, the motion of the earth around him having faded.

The taxi burned brightly, and he shuddered at the thought of the burning driver, though thankfully he was dead. Ryan didn't want to think about a world where death could be a blessing. He could have been trapped in that car, trapped in the flames. Fire, his worst fear; his nightmare.

Living, breathing fire tracked steadily on its way up the hillside following a dirty trail of oil and fuel that speeded its path. He really needed to move and *now,* but for a second, he stopped, still dazed, still watching LA shattered by the ground on which it had risen. *Jesus, this looks worse than the Northridge quake of '94.* That quake had only lasted thirty seconds, but he remembered it killed sixty people and injured several thousand. Images of collapsed freeways and fires flashed across his thoughts, quick jumbled images of death and destruction. This looked bad, but this wasn't a small part of the city. The entire downtown of LA looked to be destroyed.

Below him lay LA, and around him, but not too near, he heard sirens and smelled the odor of smoke. Nathan was somewhere above him, perhaps hit as hard as he'd been. Maybe he was trapped, possibly dead— Ryan froze and refused to think any more of the worst scenario.

Should he try to contact someone? Who? Emergency services? If the situation hadn't been so horrendous, Ryan might have laughed at the stupidity of his thought. There was no one else that could be right here and now; Nathan had him and him alone to depend upon.

He checked his pocket. Shit, his cell was in the car.

Tensing his muscles one by one, he tested for injuries. Each limb seemed bruised but worked. Nothing appeared broken, and he was relatively uninjured. His breathing had become easy and regular. He thanked the heavens for the fact that he went running every day and was fit. Picking his way carefully, he started up the hill. Climbing over piles of stone and tossed trees and foliage, he managed to trace parts of the broken road, breaking into a run when he could. He'd been running for ten minutes when he came to an abrupt stop.

"Holy shit."

Mother Nature had destroyed all that Ryan knew as right and normal. The road twisted in on itself, decimated and ripped apart. It was difficult to see where he needed to scramble but as long as he moved uphill, he was going in the right direction. He imagined he was just over two miles from Nathan's apartment, in normal circumstances about twenty minutes at a steady uphill run. Over the unsettled wasteland, he traversed, knowing the trip would last much longer.

Nathan could be hurt up there. Over the next rise could be total devastation. Ryan quickened his jog, his heart pounding as he jumped and climbed the fallen hillside. He didn't pass any other cars that had signs of life in them, just burned, twisted wreckage and bodies he couldn't stand to look at.

As he topped the last hill, to the place where Nathan's complex had sat, he stopped, horrified. He gaped at a scene that looked like something out of a war movie. Everything was flat. Half the mountain had crushed the private entrance. The gates and what had been the parking area were torn in two.

"Jesus."

CHAPTER 3

It was the coughing and the moaning that pushed Nathan to consciousness, and it took him a few desperate minutes to realize it was him making the noises.

Earthquake.

A bad one if the destruction around him was anything to go by. He couldn't see much farther than he could reach. The masonry dust drifted around him heavily, and the ground still shook beneath him, dislodging cement and bricks. He could see light above him, daylight where there should be another apartment. *Shit this must be bad, really bad.*

He knew the apartment was empty, had been empty since Christmas, but the sky... That didn't seem right. It wasn't right.

He reached out with one hand, trying to gauge what he could feel, what he could understand of the debris around him, but his movement was limited and the ground was still moving. It was surreal, frightening, and he could feel the edges of panic start to cloud his thoughts as he tested his extremities and realized he couldn't move his legs. Heavy steel lay across his hip and down past his knees. Breathing slowly and deeply, he pushed at the steel, but he may as well be pushing a solid wall for all it gave under his attempts. In fact, all it did was raise more choking dust.

He decided to lie still, very still, until the earth stopped moving and the dust settled, maybe wait for emergency services. They wouldn't be far. They wouldn't take long; they'd be here soon. The closest person that knew he was here was Jason, and he was in downtown LA, quite a few miles from here. So, shit, he needed to let his out-of-state contacts know what had happened so that they would stop worrying.

His cell. If he could get to his cell in the left pocket of his sweats... He could maybe tell Jason where he was, that he needed help, talk to his brother as well. He pushed his hand down, feeling his way, not even sure how far his hand was from the pocket, just knowing with enough grim determination he would get to the cell.

He could feel the cell, feel it in his pocket, the outline of it, but *shit*. The material was bunched, and he couldn't get it out. Frustration made him whimper. This was not good, and he started pulling at the seam, desperate to reach inside. Picking, pulling trying to ease the material apart. The ground had stopped shaking, and a sudden peace surrounded him that was unnatural. He heard no noises at all, and he held in a breath in anticipation of any sound at all, not wanting to move and miss it, as if any movement could be the death of him.

Nathan had managed to pick his way through to the inner lining of the pocket, cursing Nike for their fucking stitching. The pain in his legs was numbing, and he knew that was a bad sign. He had realized straight away that he couldn't sit up, and a combination of twisted steel and masonry made the space he was lying in impossibly small. He could still see the daylight, the early morning light spilling in to cast eerie shadows over his limited space. Taking stock of the situation, he knew two things for certain; he wasn't going anywhere under his own steam and aftershocks were inevitable.

He knew there was very little between his fragile human body and the remains of his apartment torn apart by the forces of Nature. He prayed to God that the shifting earth echoes didn't dislodge the steel that was holding together his cocoon of safety.

He had heard his cell ring, the unique ring he had for his brother, Adam. He wanted to shout "I'm here, I'm okay, someone help me." He just needed to get to the phone. Ease the threads apart...pull...pull...ease them apart, visualize the seam. His hand slowly made its way in, and he moaned in relief as his cramped fingers closed around his cell. He couldn't move his arm enough to see the phone, but he keyed speed dial from memory and hit speaker phone. His brother's voice was instant and threaded with fear.

"Nathan, what the fuck, the news… Are you okay?"

"Adam." Nathan knew his voice sounded small. It echoed in the silence around him. He needed to push his voice, use what he knew from acting and project his desperation and need for help.

"Nathan, for fuck's sake—"

"Adam, I need help…trapped, man."

"Shit. Fuck. In the apartment?"

"Yeah."

"I'm on it Nathan. Hold on." He heard Adam talking, to his wife, to his family, to… his mom? Why would his mom—

"Nathan, Dad is calling this in. Hang tight, little brother. They've added your name and location."

"My cell." Nathan whimpered softly, hoping no one heard his fear. "I can't stay— s'battery…"

"Nathan, can you tell me what you see, what you know?"

"Light, I can see…light…trapped…steel and concrete…I think the rest is gone, Adam. I can see light."

"Okay, man, save the cell, help is on the way."

Soon, please, Adam, soon.

* * * *

Fear thick in his throat, Ryan clambered down broken floors and through smashed glass, his bare skin tearing on exposed masonry and steel. Only a small part of the apartment had survived. The top floor had sheared off and lay in pieces. He had already found one body— a young woman, a brunette. She'd looked to simply be sleeping, but clearly she was gone from this world, because he felt for a pulse and found nothing. She was surrounded by photos and linens —life— but there was nothing he could do for her. She was way past any kind of help he could provide.

He tried to visualize where Nathan's apartment had been on the lower south corner facing the garden, but the whole complex had slid, crumbling and snapping and tearing as it was swallowed by the hungry earth. There was only a small part of the structure left, buried in mud and debris, and Ryan only had one hope— to find his ex-lover alive and unharmed.

He slid the last few meters to a pile of stones and wood— a fireplace. Electric cables twisted and popped as they snaked and touched each other, and carefully he picked his way to the final structure standing. He recognized nothing, no photos, no decoration, nothing that marked this as Nathan's in any way, but he knew somehow that this was Nathan's apartment. Knew? More like hoped— prayed.

Glass from a smashed window sliced into his hand, and he yelped as it dug and twisted into him. He stopped, pulling the glass out carefully, blood oozing to the surface. Distracted, he wiped it on his jeans, and judging where he stood, he carefully made his way into the sculpture of steel.

"Nathan…Nathan." *Come on, man, please be here somewhere. Please still be alive.* "Nathan, Nathan, Nathan," he repeated over and over, picking his way past doorframes and kitchen cupboards forced open under pressure, spilling cans and crockery onto the floor. It was strangely intimate seeing the contents thrown and smashed around him, imagining them lined up carefully in the cupboard, Nathan putting them away, his gentle touches, his pride in his possessions, destroyed in seconds. He moved slowly over the broken cupboards, calling Nathan's name, stumbling, trying not to knock anything that might cause a mini landslide.

He stopped, realizing he was making so much noise that he wouldn't hear if Nathan was there, trapped under the rubble. He had to stop panicking. He had to go against his instinct to scream and shout and just stand still.

"Nathan? Nathan?"

* * * *

Nathan gripped the cell like a lifeline. Adam knew he was trapped; Adam would try and get help for him. He just needed to wait. He coughed; he tried not to, but his throat was lined with dust, and it was getting damned difficult to breathe.

"Nathan, Nathan."

Jeez, now he was hallucinating. Ryan's voice. But Ryan was in New York; Ryan wasn't here.

Ryan was probably with the brunette he'd taken up with. Of course Nathan had known Ryan was bi and that there had been a woman in his past, this Allison woman, but Ryan had chosen Nathan, hadn't he? He really thought that in Ryan he'd found the man he could possibly spend the rest of his life with, which made the betrayal all the more painful.

It was stupid that he even began to think of the one thing he could never have, over and above all the other things he should be focusing on. Like survival. He really expected to die here. It was a remote location, time wasn't on his side, and he had no feeling in his legs. What did it say that this close to death all he could imagine was the panicked voice of his lover? The same man that refused to show love and compassion for its own sake, who wanted to own him, to possess him, not to share himself. He was seriously losing it big time.

He heard the voice again. "Nathan, Nathan."

"Stop it, leave me alone," Nathan said softly to himself. If he was going to die, it wasn't going to be with Ryan's panicked voice and memories of their last argument in his head. He wanted to focus on their friendship, on the love he had for him, not when it was all screwed to hell. He wanted to think about his family.

CHAPTER 4

Ryan heard something— words. *Stop it. Alone.* Nathan.

Desperately he scrabbled under bent beams, dodging dislodged brick and stone. It was hard to make sense of what he was seeing, everything upside down, walls collapsed, ceiling and floor mixed in rubble and dust. There was no visible sign of his ex-lover, and he had almost lost all hope, standing in silence, trying to hear something— anything. A sound, a movement, and finally he could track it to a large steel beam that pinned Nathan down to the hard floor.

"Oh God, oh God, no," he stammered falling to his knees.

It was difficult to make out Nathan's features with his eyes closed and covered in gray dust. Ryan stared, shocked for a few moments, then reality kicked him back, and shaking, he reached for Nathan's neck, locating a fluttering pulse. Still alive. He let out the breath that he didn't even realize he'd been holding, a sigh of relief. He dropped his head nearer to Nathan's face, feeling his breath, and touching a shaking hand to his forehead. He was unconscious but alive. As Ryan considered what to do, where to start, Nathan's eyes opened suddenly, an intense green against his gray dusty face. Ryan rocked back on his heels in sudden surprise.

"Nathan, oh my God, what hurts? Where are you hurt?"

Nathan didn't say anything in return. His unfocused eyes looked directly at Ryan, then blinked. He frowned, then it seemed to make sense, and his eyes widened as he coughed, starting to bring his head up to Ryan.

"Adam," he rasped, lifting his hand as much as he could. Ryan saw the imprint of the cellphone keys in his flesh. His voice was so quiet, but Ryan understood what he meant— tell his family that he was with Nathan, that Nathan wasn't alone.

There was a signal, but the battery was low, and he tried not to focus on the fact that probably hundreds, even thousands, of people were trying to get through to loved ones and the network would be overloaded. He thumbed through the contacts, located Adam, and keyed the name, holding it to his ears, his palm resting flat on Nathan's head as he lowered it back to the cold stone floor. He was examining the area around his friend while the cell tried to connect. It took five tries, and Ryan sent his thanks skyward that it had actually connected. He knew what he needed to ask. He needed to know what the situation was with emergency services, what was happening in LA.

"Nathan?"

"No. Adam, it's Ryan, I'm here with Nathan. Battery's low."

"What are you—"

"I was outside when it hit. Tell me what's going on, Adam."

"Fire, in the hills, spreading towards LA. You need to get away from the apartment, Ryan. I'm serious."

"What about emergency services?"

"Running evac. CNN is showing massive damage downtown. They're worried about aftershocks, but the fire in the hills, Ryan, the fire is the worst. It's spreading downwind to LA, right where you are."

"We're going now, trust me," and then saying no more, he closed the cell, not wanting to waste the battery. What was the point in explaining in detail that it seemed that Nathan was trapped for the duration? No point at all.

He pocketed the cell, then started to feel around Nathan's trapped limbs. It seemed it was just the one beam that had landed and pinned him from right thigh to his left ankle with no room to move. The beam was twisted and buried deep in a mountain of rubble and debris, and for the life of him, he couldn't see how he was going to move the damn thing. He tried putting two hundred twenty pounds of gym-honed muscle into pushing it off, but that only elicited a groaning from the structure and a frightened demand to stop from Nathan, who was clearly in pain.

"Nathan, tell me where it hurts," Ryan said softly, kneeling at Nathan's side, cradling a hand into dark blond hair.

"Pushing on…chest, ribs, now…it hurt my legs…but no more…I can't feel my legs." Nathan's barely there voice rose on a panicked note, and Ryan had to think on his feet.

"They're just numb, Nathan. The beam is resting on you; it's just cutting off the circulation."

"Swear to me, Ry."

"I swear." Ryan hoped he came across as firm and convincing. He didn't know for one minute why Nathan couldn't feel his legs, but he hoped to God he was right and that it was just pressure on them. "We need to get this off of you. I need to make a…" He couldn't think of the word— something to pivot, to push off the steel. He realized Nathan had said nothing else, and that the man's eyes had closed again. Damn it, he needed to stay conscious. "Nathan, talk to me, Nathan."

"M'really tired." Nathan's voice was slurring, a combination of exhaustion and shock, and his limbs and torso were trembling visibly.

"Stay with me, Nathan. When I get this off you

need to slide out. You need to brace yourself. Can you do that? Nathan... Nathan?" He watched as Nathan pushed with his hands, but it was no use whatsoever. He didn't have the upper body strength to push himself out, not with possibly cracked ribs and all sorts of other hidden injuries. Ryan certainly wasn't going to dissuade the positive attempt though. "That's good, Nathan, just stay still for me. We'll get you out."

Again Ryan pushed, but nothing was happening. He forced his entire strength against the steel, hoping for a break, hoping the thing would move enough to drag Nathan free. Almost sobbing with the exertion and frustration of it not moving, and completely defeated, he slumped down, touching Nathan's forehead, listening as Nathan mumbled something incoherent. He lowered his ear to Nathan's mouth. His eyes caught the water bottle that he imagined Nathan had been holding. Somehow it was still intact and a quarter full, and he dribbled some water into Nathan's mouth. Water was good. He'd read that somewhere; water is always good.

Nathan coughed then spoke, forcing out words, staccato and urgent.

"Ground...not right...can feel..." The ground?

Ryan understood even as the ground started to move again, subtly rolling under them. It was another shake, and

Ryan immediately thought of aftershocks as the entire apartment structure shifted again. Still it was enough to crack supports, and part of the ceiling started to fall. Ryan didn't think. He threw himself on top of Nathan, protecting his head and praying this wasn't the end. The ground shifting grew in intensity, shaking loose any item that had wedged in the main quake, and dropping it onto the two men.

"Don't," Nathan tried to say over the noise of the falling debris. "You gotta leave, Ry, this is stupid. One of us…"

Ryan tensed as rocks and pieces of rubble crashed down on them, onto his back. He didn't hear Nathan cry out at all, and Ryan waited until blessed peace came at last, following a few groans in the structure and settling debris. Ryan lifted his head, not even thinking of the injuries that had just cut into him, more focused on how the new tremor may have affected Nathan's position.

"Nathan, I think I can… I can see space here."

Space where there was none before. There was a clear gap now between the steel and Nathan's legs. He crouched low and tensed his leg muscles to give him solid purchase, and immediately tried to pull Nathan, but nothing happened.

"Nathan, I need you to help me. Can you help me?

Relax, let me pull you out." He got a good grip under Nathan's arms, his own hands wet with blood, and pulled, heaving, digging his heels in, and finally, slowly, Nathan moved from under the twisted steel. There was no time for self-congratulation, no time to stop and rest. They needed to get out of here before the next aftershock. The structure about them was precarious at best, hanging on by a few beams and little else.

With the impetus of fear and the adrenaline of action, Ryan lifted Nathan as best he could. Ryan might be built, and he might work out every day, but shit, Nathan was no lightweight. A lifeless man in shock was not an easy burden to carry.

"Help me, Nathan, help me —come on— we need to get out of here —daylight— we need some air— come on." Each word was punctuated with another step towards the hill outside what was left of the apartment complex. Exhausted and drained, Ryan finally slumped to the brown summer grass, sliding Nathan gently to the ground.

"Nathan." Ryan leaned over him, anxiously poking at his leg and seeing it twitch. He had never felt so relieved. They were outside, they were both alive, and everything was okay. The pain in his back was now a dull ache, but he needed to see what was there, needed Nathan's help to see if anything was open and needed attention. Thing was

Nathan was lying on the ground, gasping for air, moving his legs, reaching down to touch his chest.

"Ribs?" Ryan asked gently. Nathan opened his eyes and nodded, his eyes glazed and his face creased in a frown.

"Yeah, can't breathe so well," he said simply, "but that is nothing compared to the whole leg…shit, my ankle, I…" He subsided into silence.

"Can you stand, Nathan? We need to make a move."

"I need some time, just need to catch a fucking breath."

"We can't stay."

"I can't go anywhere. Shit, Ry, we need to stay and wait for help."

"Adam said there are fires up on the ridge, behind us, so we need to move. Move down, 'cus they're coming this way." Ryan swore as Nathan visibly paled, fully aware of what he had just revealed, that Nathan had been trapped in the path of a forest fire above LA.

* * * *

"Fuck." Nathan struggled to stand, his ankle on fire, his legs not really letting him stand on his own, pains shooting through him as the blood started to flow more evenly through his body.

Ryan was up in an instant, helping him, linking his hands around Nathan's back, Nathan swayed for a moment, his hands coming to rest on Ryan's lower back, slipping and sliding against wet material. He finally grabbed a handful of material that gave him purchase. Ryan was obviously trying not to grimace, urging Nathan to lean against the twisted gate to the park area.

"Turn the fuck round," Nathan bit out, looking down at blood on his hands, seeing the fresh red on him.

Ryan winced at the harshness in Nathan's words but turned nonetheless. "Ryan fuck—your back is shredded."

"Is it bad?"

"Aren't you in pain?"

"Nathan, is it bad, bleeding badly?"

"More of an ooze than a gush," he finally said.

"Then it'll be fine; we will be fine."

"Shit, Ryan, it's… You need to get to a—"

"Nathan, shut the fuck up. If it's not bleeding badly then we don't have to do anything with it. We walk."

Walk? Easy for him to say, but Nathan did try, the pain in his ankle causing him to limp badly. He had to stop frequently and retch into the grass.

* * * *

Ryan stopped, but the need to move allowed no patience for Nathan being sick. He resorted to taking

Nathan's weight against him and slowly they made their way farther from the complex. Nathan suddenly stopped, turning back to look at the devastation.

"Angie... She was... we need to find her... this morning, she waved at me."

"Young girl, brunette?" Ryan swallowed as he realized he had already found the girl.

"Yeah, pretty, actress."

"Sorry, man, she's gone." There was no other way to say it.

"Gone."

"Yeah. Is there anyone else here?" Ryan asked. But inside he knew they had to go, and if it came to a choice of rescuing others or getting Nathan down off of this damn mountain of destruction, then there really was no question as to what he would do.

"We should go and..." Nathan was rambling, pain bracketing his mouth as he attempted to turn back to look at the crushed apartment block. "We should get Angie to...her body...just away from the fire."

"She's gone, man. I checked her myself. There is nothing else we can do. Was there anyone else there?"

Nathan shook his head as if he could clear his head of the horror. "No, just the two apartments out of the five, just me and Angie and Oscar."

"Oscar?" Shit. There was someone else? Ryan glanced at the destruction that had once been a beautiful styled complex. Surely no one else could have survived that.

"Dog, stray, kinda hangs out round the area." Ryan breathed a sigh of relief.

"He'll have been long gone, man. Dogs sense these things."

"Yeah…the birds." Nathan looked a bit spaced out, and Ryan snapped his fingers in front of Nathan's face, trying to bring him back to the present. "We need to leave Angie? Are you sure?" Nathan finally stuttered.

"I'm sorry, but please, we need to get away from here and down the side. We need to get to safety." He didn't realize just how much he was begging for them to just get a move on.

Nathan didn't say anything else, just leaned into Ryan's supporting hold and together they started to move downhill.

There was a steady noise in the distance, coming closer, a *thwump thwump*, and four black as night helicopters flew overhead, down the hill towards downtown LA. Neither man said a word, and neither acknowledged that the army was now clearly involved in whatever had happened below.

"I think I saw LA," Ryan finally murmured, more to hear noise than to actually speak. "I saw it when I got here. It was burning, there were…fires…and clouds of dust, debris— buildings at crazy angles."

"Jason is down there. He was in a Starbucks, I'd only just gotten off the phone talking to him," Nathan said softly.

"Your friend from the show?" Ryan asked without his customary vitriol at the other man in Nathan's life. "I'm sure he'll be okay. I mean the whole thing happened really early. He'll have been in the open; he'll be fine."

Ryan wasn't convinced about what he was saying. After all, he'd seen the proud skyline broken and drunken in destruction. He didn't vocalize his fears and doubts— it was hard enough to walk, let alone worry about a situation in the city below that was way beyond his help.

CHAPTER 5

They stumbled some distance before they smelled the smoke. Neither wanted to turn round to see what they feared was behind them.

"We gotta step this up," Ryan urged. "Can you walk faster?"

Nathan swallowed; he was already pushing it to walk at this pace. Every movement crunched something in his ankle, and his breathing was labored. He knew *he* couldn't go any faster, but Ryan could. Ryan could run ahead, get out of the way of the fire, get help, maybe he could get back here in time?

"Ryan, I can't. I really am trying, but you need to go ahead and get help."

"You need me to help you walk. I'm not going ahead."

"You could get help."

"I'd never get back up in time, and they're dealing with a city in flames. They won't be focusing on the hills."

Nathan was tired and in pain. Why couldn't Ryan see this and just leave him to sit on the side of what was left of the road. "Ryan, just go, I'll—"

Ryan spun so fast Nathan almost lost his footing, and he was suddenly hauled up against a desperate-eyed

Ryan, his face inches away.

"Fuck you, Nathan. I didn't leave you to burn in your apartment. Do you think I'm gonna leave you to burn now?"

They stared at each other, Nathan's breath hitching, the pain in his chest flaring. Whatever Ryan's faults, he wouldn't leave anyone to burn alive. He would save whoever needed to be saved, not just Nathan.

"I just don't want to hold you up," Nathan said, wheezing.

Ryan relaxed, the fight leaving him as quickly as it arrived. "I'm not leaving you," he finished simply, and with this declaration from Ryan, they resumed their slow journey downhill, Nathan still itching to make Ryan go ahead, not wanting to hold him back.

Nathan really was trying so hard to walk faster, but the pain in his ankle— the grating, the sharp insistent break as he walked— added to the whole not being able to breathe thing— was making it impossible to push any more. Ryan was supporting as much weight as he could, but Jesus, he wasn't Superman, and frustration that he wouldn't leave him and go ahead was bubbling insistently below the surface.

This was typical. Damn stubborn, irritating, controlling, insufferable man. Always in control, always organizing, always so anal about detail. Nathan swore Ryan had OCD when it came to stubbornness and control.

Well, Nathan wasn't ready for that. Nathan was his own man, and he could organize his own life, thank you very much. He didn't need the Ortiz rules to live by. He didn't need jealousy, and he didn't need to be told what to do.

Fuck, he really loved the big idiot. Why couldn't Ryan share, trust his lover? Didn't he know him well enough to know Nathan would never hurt him? And was that really the problem? Shit, why was he considering this when he should be focusing on getting down to civilization, or what was left of it.

Nathan could imagine the fire. He'd seen the images on CNN from the last one. He'd sat with Ryan as they watched it get close to his apartment, worried with him, then sighed in relief when the fire turned, so close, only a quarter of a mile away. The smoke was visible now. Wisps floated around them, a breeze following them down the hills, bringing with it a forewarning of the destruction that would follow. Each time a disaster happened— the fires, earthquakes, hurricanes— it felt remote and removed on the news, not like this, not personal and vindictive.

They had been stumbling downhill for at least an hour when Nathan heard the barking long before he actually saw the scruffy mutt.

"Oscar," he breathed softly. The dog that hung around the apartment building looking for scraps stood on an outcrop of broken and torn road, barking insistently.

"That's Oscar?" Ryan said. They stopped. Ryan tried to call him over, but the dog stubbornly stood where he was, his ears pricked, and his tail high. "Is he normally this active?"

"Nah, he's usually kinda quiet," Nathan confirmed. "Can you grab him, Ry?"

Ryan left Nathan propped against a fallen tree and crossed to the dog, who danced backwards and down the side of the twisted road.* * * *

Ryan made himself look as small as he could, stooping low to approach the dog as it danced backward, woofing softly and whining again.

"Wassup, boy, are we heading for a new aftershock, huh? Is that what you're tryin' to tell us?" Oscar whined and turned, jumping off of the outcrop and disappearing.

Ryan almost ignored him and crossed back to Nathan. If Oscar was warning of an aftershock then Nathan would need help just to stand, let alone to handle the earth moving. But something, some instinct to trust this barking dog, made Ryan turn back and scramble up the six foot ribbon of twisted road, looking down at where Oscar had disappeared and to a scene of carnage he would remember until the day he died.

Five cars, thrown from the road. Two were burned out, with shadows of people inside. Two other cars had been crushed by road and rubble, and one car, like his taxi, had been half cut and pressed to nothing with huge rocks and chunks of road leaning precariously over it. Was anyone alive? Why was Oscar leading him down there? He wasn't sure he could handle this.

"Daddy, doggy," a small voice said. The sound was so small Ryan almost missed it and it came, from the car cut in half. Calling back to Nathan, he clambered down the other side of the newly exposed earth and climbed over God knows what to get to the car at the front.

"Hello?" he said. He couldn't see through the spider web of broken glass

"Daddy?"

Shit, a child was in there. He tried to move round to see in, finally finding a small part of the car that offered a glance inside. A little girl sat in a car seat, untouched, but with the belts twisted and stuck. The only way to get her out was to remove the broken glass.

"Hey, darlin', I'm Ryan. I'm here to help. Can you cover your eyes, sweetie? I need to break the glass." As soon as she moved her hands, he pushed the glass in, trying to ignore her shrieks of fear. Reaching in, he pulled at the belt, untwisting it and grabbing at the girl, pulling her out in one move. She was so tiny, no older than his three-year-old niece.

He heard Oscar whining, his gut instinct telling him that the dog wanted him to move. He was convinced that another aftershock was building under his feet, and desperately he moved away from the cars, the little girl sobbing into his neck, hanging on for dear life. He made it to the top of the rubble pile, sliding and slipping towards Nathan as another aftershock pulled at the earth, the hill that was left collapsing and crushing the girl's car. He felt sick. He hadn't been able to tell if her parents had been in the car. There'd been nothing left of the front half of the car when he got there, and there was certainly nothing of it left at all now.

"Ryan, Jesus," was all Nathan could say. "What the—"

Ryan just shook his head. *Don't ask questions, just leave it.* "We need to keep walking." He switched the little girl to his left side. He winced as her small hands twisted into the back of his torn shirt, pulling at open wounds. He gritted his teeth, then wrapped his right hand around Nathan. "Let's walk."

The smell of fire was overwhelming here, but Ryan

couldn't tell if that was because of the burning cars or if it was the specter of death sweeping down the hill as they descended, trying to grab at the few survivors on the side of this mountain. He tried to quicken the pace. He couldn't even ask the little girl her name, because it made it too personal. What if he had a name to put to his failure to keep them alive. He couldn't handle that. What if he failed?

* * * *

CNN ran the same reel over and over, the devastation in LA, the iconic buildings and landmarks, some ripped in half, fire destroying the rest, estimates of thousands dead. The President issued a federal disaster declaration, the army was in control, and a swarm of helicopters ferried people and medical help to and from the epicenter. It didn't seem real. There were stories, stories of survival, miraculous escapes from destroyed buildings, even as an aftershock sent emergency services workers to their deaths as they struggled to help.

Adam didn't know what to say as they watched. They could do nothing. They had told the Ortizes that their son had contacted them. Ryan's family had thought he was safe in New York. It was the hardest call that Adam had ever made to tell them otherwise.

The fires in the hills had merged, causing one huge forest fire, and emergency services from twelve different states had volunteered, joining the search and rescue crews, fighting fires and helping with looting control. It was a vision of hell that had been foretold since the San Francisco quake of 1906, but one that people chose to not think about.

It was real.

CHAPTER 6

The smoke was no longer a suggestion or a maybe. It was starting to get into the air they were breathing, and in their noses. Ryan did his best to hide the little girl's face in his neck, urging her to breathe gently, and with his other arm, he attempted to support Nathan more, hearing the rasping in his chest, knowing he must be in so much pain.

Every so often he looked back. The last time he saw the fire jumping from treetop to treetop at the top of the hill, his imagination hearing the spits, and the crackle and the roar of the fire eating away at everything in its path.

He knew it was a mile, maybe less, to the base of the hill and to the highway. Surely there would be something there, some kind of rescue for those people like them that had been trapped on the side of the hills. Surely the highway would provide a natural break for the fire. If he could just get Nathan and the girl to the other side...

He saw more cars, tossed like children's toys to the side, mostly empty, some with people —bodies— with no life in their eyes. Ryan couldn't bear to look, wondering how these nightmare images would visit him when they were safe.

He heard a voice. "Help, help me."

No, I can't hear that, I can't, hold Nathan closer,

hide the girl's face.

"Please, man, just pull me out, please."

Nathan stopped. Ryan couldn't bring himself to not look. He saw a man trapped in the car, his face covered in blood.

The man's face was twisted in agony. A woman lay dead in the seat beside him, and the specter of the fire behind them danced, sending pinpoints of light onto the black polished metal of the car. Weighing his options — keep moving or leave a man to die— Ryan didn't hesitate. He placed the child on the ground and helped Nathan to stand. He instinctively pulled on the door handle of the distorted car. It wouldn't move, but with no glass in the way, he leaned in over the body of the dead woman whose eyes were wide, frozen in horror. He could hear the man's voice, broken and scared.

Ryan leaned in closer, cataloguing the extent of the damage. The engine had been forced back into the car, leaving the passenger dead and the driver, the man, with his legs trapped and mangled.

He would have to pull the man free, but he could see there was no way. Even the fire department with jaws of life would take longer than he had. Tears pushed at his eyes, angry frustrated tears, and he pulled back abruptly to return to Nathan, starting to slide an arm under his friend to resume the walk.

"Wait, we need to—" Nathan coughed, and Ryan lifted his chin, looking deep into green eyes wide with horror.

"I can't help him; there's no time. I have to get you and the girl to safety," he said clearly, feeling his stomach churn and heave at the thought that he was condemning a man to die.

"Tell him we'll send help. Please…"

Ryan's heart twisted. He knew what he needed to do. He needed to be hard, focused, but Nathan stood with agony carved into his face.

"Okay, I'll tell him." He crossed over the twisted road, clambering to the car, trying to get his head round this, pulling on every skill of pretense he had.

The man gasped, "You gotta help me."

"I'm Ryan," he said softly. "I can't get you out, man. We're gonna send someone back for you, okay?" The man looked relieved. He coughed, blood flecks spewing around his mouth. "You'll be okay, man, we'll get you help." He raised a hand, gripping Ryan's in a blood-covered hold.

"David— Jackson, thanks."

Ryan pulled his hand free, stumbling back towards Nathan in horror at what he'd just done. There would be no time for David Jackson; the fire would be here before they could get someone.

He couldn't think, couldn't even begin to process the horror of what he'd just had to do, of the decision he'd made. He lifted the little girl, who looked confused, hoping to God that she wouldn't remember any of this if she lived through the day, and he grasped Nathan securely, encouraging his exhausted ex to walk.

It was all Ryan could do to center on what was happening, but every thought focused on Allison. What would she tell their child? If he died here, how would she explain it?

The guilt was eating him away inside, and he still hadn't told Nathan that his ex-girlfriend was pregnant with his child. Hadn't been *able* to tell Nathan. He needed to. Shit. If they were gonna die here, if they couldn't make it out, the smoke killing them, the fire leaving no trace that they were even here, he needed to talk to Nathan at some point, to make it somehow right. He didn't stop to talk; he couldn't. The smoke was thick in his lungs, his head fuzzy.

Nathan rasped, clinging tighter to Ryan's arm and squeezing as hard as he could. Ryan prayed it would be okay; they just needed to get down to the highway, to the bottom. Serious discussions could wait— Ryan would explain about Allison and the baby when they were safe.

Winds could cause the fire conditions to change by

the second, by the minute, and he knew they had very little time.

* * * *

Nathan had watched as Ryan reassured the driver, cursing his choice of apartments. The building had been so bloody remote, so far away, and then as he imagined a burning LA, he felt a stark relief that he did live outside the inner circle.

The pain eating away at Nathan's reserves was leaving him unable to coherently think about anything. It was step after step after painful step, and more and more, he was leaning into Ryan. He tried not to think about the man in the car, about the girl's parents, about the fire. He tried not to think about friends in LA, in the city... But he had only seen Jason a few days ago— he had to believe he was alright.

Ryan had said he'd seen LA burning, twisted. Jason was somewhere out there, somewhere in that carnage, in the center of a possibly destroyed city, and he desperately wanted to go back to yesterday and tell him to run. Now he wanted Ryan to run, take the girl, and run. Ryan said he wouldn't leave him, but the child... That changed things, didn't it? Now, Ryan had someone else, a child to think about.

"What's her name?" Nathan wheezed suddenly as if

it was vital to him to know the little girl. The need to run had stripped Nathan of the niceties. Something in him was making him want to know her name before the fire caught up with them and they died. Ryan asked her gently, and she murmured something in return.

"Laurie," Ryan repeated, and she nodded.

"How old are you, Laurie?"

She held up three fingers and then hid in his neck again. Laurie. Three. Ryan had made the right decision to grab her from the car. They needed to get her off of this mountain.

* * * *

Jason had been one of the lucky ones. He'd been on an early morning coffee run when the quake hit and not in his building. The building that was no longer there. Everything he owned was in his apartment. Every memory he'd built was destroyed, but when he thought of his neighbors, none of whom could have made it out alive, material possessions meant nothing. He had followed the general evacuation, moving north, trying his family and Nathan's cell repeatedly, but literally having no luck getting through. People scrambled around him, all trying numbers on cell phones, cursing at no signals. Most were shocked and panicked, some just standing in the street, blind in the dust that choked lungs.

He knew he had to get away from the center of the city, out to the suburbs. To Nathan. He should try and get to Nathan, up in the hills, north of the city. It had to be safer there.

The crowd stopped at a designated evac point, as far away from the tallest skyscrapers as they could. An hour of half running, half stumbling brought them away from the worst of the fires; they were the lucky ones. An officer with a bullhorn called for calm. Army-uniformed men with masks mingled in amongst dazed civilians.

Jason tried to hear, moving to the edge of the crowd, but still he couldn't hear enough to have any idea of what was going on. He caught a few words over the whimpering and crying and stunned disbelief that hung in the air around him.

"Fires."

Jason heard the tail end of a man speaking behind him He turned and saw an army uniform speaking into a radio, his face streaked with dust and cuts "—need to get people south. We have forest fires on the hills to the north. We'd be sending people there to die— south."

Jason didn't wait to hear more. Nathan was in the hills. What if he was trapped, what if the fires were… Nah, south was no good. What the fuck? North was where it was at, and slipping easily past the crowd in all the confusion and noise and past the army sentries herding people south of the city, he started his way north and to his friend.

* * * *

CNN had changed the story. The core of it focused on the destruction in LA, but there were sensationalist reports of mortality statistics, eyewitness accounts, and information releases from the president and the governor. New, though, was the closure of two freeways north of Los Angeles and the manner in which the fires were being dealt with. Authorities had dispatched water-dropping helicopters, and there were more than two hundred fire engines as the blaze started to push towards the city.

The camera focused on an Officer Barlow of the LA County Fire Department, and he spoke in clipped clear tones.

"About three hundred and fifty police officers are on the scene, patrolling evacuated neighborhoods and warning residents ahead of the flames."

"Nathan isn't dead," Adam said, his arms crossed, his voice calm. "I know he isn't; I would feel if he was." He said this for his momma as she sat, still as stone, transfixed by the disaster unfolding before her eyes.

Really all he could feel was dread. And knowing Nathan was alive? He wished he could feel as convinced as he tried to sound.

CHAPTER 7

The fire was coming on fast, and already it was beginning to throw shadows. The air around them had become hot and oppressive, and it seemed as if there was a reflection of fire that only Ryan could see. Smoke —sickly sour, redolent with the smell of creosote— hung around them, and danger felt uncomfortably near.

Nathan stumbled with a barely hidden shout of pain, pulling Ryan down, and Ryan, twisting at the last moment so Laurie wasn't squashed, ended up facing back up the rise, fascinated for seconds by the impassable wall of fire that was eating its way down the hillside. There were two separate fires, dancing, plunging and racing at each other, meeting with a roar that must have been heard miles away. The fire was so much taller than the tree line, coming on with a rush and a roar, crossing and twisting and leaping from tree to tree, each bursting into crimson towers of flame.

The eerie quiet of the last few hours had changed, and the sounds had become a living, horrible noise of hissing and roaring flames. The crashing and splitting apart of falling timber was deafening, terrifying. It held Ryan immobile even as Nathan pulled himself to his feet.

"Ryan," he shouted urgently, and Ryan stood,

stumbling upright and coughing.

The quality of the light had changed. The smoke covered the light from the morning sun, and the clouds were tinged with a strange red hue. The sun had become red in the smoke-filled sky. Ryan swore he could feel the heat at the back of his neck. He found himself ducking when water-dropping helicopters swooped over their head towards the heart of the chasing fire. They wouldn't have been seen, because the black copters were moving too fast to spot two men in the smoke below them as they swept over.

They must be close to the road. They must be by now.

Nathan stumbled again, pulling on Ryan's back, causing him to grunt in pain, shifting his balance to take more weight. Nathan shook his head, *sorry*, and tried to right himself, straightening his back and groaning as his ankle had weight put on it.

It was Ryan who saw them first, thin shadows in the smoke, moving closer and closer. Police uniforms. Neon yellow jackets. Help.

* * * *

Laurie wouldn't let emergency service touch her.

She clung to Ryan and whimpered. She would only talk to Ryan, and he wasn't ready to let her go. If he let go, she would be lost in the system, and he needed to find her family so he knew she was safe. He had already lost sight of Nathan— he had been helped off, lifted onto a makeshift stretcher, pain meds already pumping into him. Triage was checking him over.

"What do we do?" Ryan said to no one in particular, refusing to let someone look at his back. *We need to go. We can't stay here. Surely the fire is close?*

"We'll move you and the girl down to the blockade." The man directing the crowd was distracted and waving at another officer, who was writing on a board, touching his ear, listening to narrative.

"I'm not leaving without Nathan," Ryan insisted quickly.

"Your friend, yes, he's cleared to travel in the truck. Fuck. At the moment, if you're alive, you're okay to travel in the truck. You'll be assessed fully at the blockade."

"There's a car, in the hills, with a man trapped inside." Ryan turned to face the hill again. The flames looked like a wall advancing down the hill. He saw the evac teams pulling back, pulling away. He twisted back to the guy who had taken his name, but he had moved away. He was talking to a family, urging them to the evac vehicles. Ryan stopped talking, stopped explaining. David Jackson was gone, surely.

A sudden grief welled inside him, and he was only grounded as Laurie whimpered into his neck. He wasn't finished yet; he needed to get Nathan and Laurie down off of the mountain. That was what was important. He needed to close himself down and focus.

They were herded to a 4x4 with other refugees from the fire. Ryan was manhandled into the front seat with Laurie still hiding against his neck. They sat in silence. The only sound in the cabin was the disjointed noise of the radio. The ride was bumpy and precarious at times on the fractured road, the fire of a city on one side, the red in the hills on the other.

No one had anything to say. They sat in numb shock, in relief, in fear.

* * * *

Jason was about a mile from the base of the hill, just before the freeway. He made it that far before he was stopped, caught, and herded away, all the time protesting that his friend was in the hills.

Frustrated, he stood at the barrier set by the fire department and the police, refusing to move, determined to at least stand as close as he could to his friend until he was found, or until all hope was lost.

Jason watched every arrival at the blockade, watched as each person was dealt with efficiently and passed on to separate teams who he assumed dealt with the varying degrees of injury or suffering.

He had counted one hundred twenty seven so far, children, parents, whole families, individuals, some crying, some stoic, some still, some in flustered panic, but no Nathan.

He had listened. He wasn't stupid, and he knew the fire was past the valley edge where Nathan had his apartment in the secluded complex with the park area and the beautiful views.

It was all gone.

The next 4x4 arrived. It was Ryan he saw first, stumbling from inside the car with something in his arms. Ryan… *What the fuck is Ryan doing here?*

Jason ducked under the cordon, ignoring the shouts of the officers in charge, and dove towards the new arrivals, calling Ryan's name, watching as the tall man's head lifted and his eyes searched for the source of his name. His gaze finally came to rest on Jason, his shoulders straightening. Jason reached his side, pulling him into a one-armed hug, pulling his arm back as he encountered wet cloth and realized it was blood-soaked.

"Ryan?" He searched Ryan's eyes, asking for a reason for the blood.

"Nathan— in the back," he said gruffly, his voice raspy and smoke damaged. Jason moved to the back door, opening it and looking in at his friend, pale, bruised, covered in blood, unconscious, as still as death.

"Jesus… fuck." He looked back at Ryan. "He's not…"

"No, we…" Ryan couldn't get the words out, and he pried away Laurie's hands, passing her protesting body to Jason, who took her without a moment's thought.

"Keep her," he whispered. "Don't let…process her… my back." Jason could see Ryan was losing it. He had felt Ryan's blood on his own hands, scarlet and fresh.

"I'll look after her." Ryan slipped to the ground against the car door.

People— doctors, officers, nurses— buzzed around them, pulling Ryan and Nathan this way and that, turning Ryan over, meaning that Jason could see his back. It was a mass of bruises and deep cuts, oozing fresh blood, the material of his shirt stuck into the wounds. He had never seen anything like it and watched in sickened amazement as the paramedics attempted to peel back the material of the shirt to irrigate the wounds. At this point, it seemed Ryan had lost consciousness. Shit, Jason was surprised he'd even made it this far.

He hovered like a mother with her baby birds, feeling Laurie relax into him inch by slow inch. The fact that Ryan had handed her to him seemed to make him someone she could trust. They tried to take her away from him, but he refused. Laurie Allen, aged three, with a Christmas birthday, was staying with her new uncle Jason, and that was that. He answered the questions that he could. He knew almost everything about Nathan, and equally hardly anything at all about Ryan.

Next of kin for Ryan? I don't know, Nathan's family may know. Can you get to them through Nathan's family? Allergies, Nathan, no, Ryan, I don't know. It was a blur. *Where are you taking them now? The hospitals in LA. Is it safe? I'm going with them, Laurie too. I'm not arguing with you, I'm going.*

The earth chose that moment to shake, a mild aftershock, sending a ripple of fear through the civilians and causing frantic movement for the rescuers. Jason was waved through without comment, climbing into the same evacuation vehicle as both Ryan and Nathan. He tried his cell phone, and the twenty-second time, he actually connected.

"Jason?"

"Adam, shit, I'm with Nathan. He's fine, he's—we're in evac. They say some broken ribs. We're moving out; I don't know where they're taking us."

"Thank God."

"Can you pass on that Ryan is with us? He's cut up quite bad, but he's here, so tell his parents and text me their contact details."

"Will it get through?"

"Fuck knows. I'm not having a—" And then static.

CHAPTER 8

They arrived at the next evacuation area to organized chaos. Jason was torn between following Ryan or Nathan, deciding instead to hover with the coordinator, Laurie still in his arms. The coordinator looked at him disapprovingly, but he stared her down. He wasn't moving. From where he stood, he could see CNN on a laptop showing the fires downtown and the evacuation, and it chilled him to the bone. It was as if he was watching a disaster movie— none of it was real.

The wind had changed, chasing the fire away from the highways, leaving devastation in its wake. Most of the downtown fires had been contained, but some were still burning. Reports of estimated death tolls were climbing every minute, five thousand, ten thousand, seventeen thousand, more. He didn't know what to focus on first. He leaned against the wall, Laurie asleep against his shoulder, even in the confusion and noise of intake.

He watched people enter Nathan's cubicle, then saw them leave half an hour later, heads together. He waited as they discussed something, then slipped inside. Nathan lay still and unmoving, his face white, his freckles in stark relief. At least his breathing was steady. Jason stood for a short while until the curtain moved, and the coordinator appeared, looking directly at him. He readied himself for a battle, but she looked exhausted and white.

"We are setting up for emergency blood donations. Can you donate, sir?"

"I can donate. I've been checked, so I can do that. Jason— I'm Jason."

* * * *

Ryan came back to consciousness far too quickly as they were still stitching the cuts and slices in his back. He cried out in pain, and apparently gave the attending doctor the fright of his life as the doc jumped back with his own cry.

"Sorry, sorry, we're short on— Jeez, fuck, just sorry."

Where's Nathan? Laurie?

"I'm done." the doctor muttered, his words slurred and edgy. Ryan pushed himself up to sit, his back literally on fire with pain. "You need to sit for at least half an hour to let the meds kick in." He handed Ryan a fresh shirt, the top half of a pair of scrubs. Ryan looked at him, his head heavy, his throat raw, and his voice fading.

"Okay." *No way, just go will you, so I can find them?*

"I'll check back on you," the young doctor said, dropping notes onto Ryan's gurney, sighing deeply, and pushing his way out of the tent.

Ryan counted to twenty and stood, shaky on his legs, but determined to find Nathan and Laurie, and within minutes, he'd checked most cubicles, finding Nathan in the second from last.

He looked really peaceful. They'd attached a drip into his arm— feeding God knows what into him, pain relief, glucose, and Ryan almost sagged in relief. Jason wasn't here, and neither was Laurie, but all of a sudden, he just wanted to sit with Nathan, touch Nathan, ground himself in the here and now. The gurney was low to the ground, and it was enough to drop to his knees next to it, dipping his forehead to the cover, and sending a quick prayer heavenwards that they made it here.

"I gave blood," a quiet voice said behind him. He turned painfully to face the owner of the voice. Jason. *Where's Laurie?* He wanted to say it, but he couldn't.

"Laurie's with the staff, the other kids. I booked her in using my name." Ryan nodded, swallowing, wanting to push out words. "Who is she, Ryan?"

"I don't know," he rasped, but it seemed important to get this information to Jason. "Found her— in a car, what was left of her car. Her family…" He couldn't say any more. None of it seemed real. Jason didn't push.

"They think Nathan's cracked a coupla ribs, but he needs X-rays, and they don't have it here. He also has a possible splintered hip bone, soft tissue damage from the hip to the knee, and a broken ankle."

Ryan looked stricken. "I made him walk," he pushed out, his throat tight and his stomach turning in self disgust.

"I don't wanna hear that, Ryan. You saved him, him and little Laurie." Ryan dismissed the comment with a grimace of pain, fighting exhaustion and fear. Why wasn't Nathan awake?

He must have said it out loud because Jason answered.

"They dosed him up to relax his breathing. He'll be coming to soon. They said he would; they promised me." Jason's voice was rough.

Ryan reached past his own pain, smiling as best he could at Nathan's best friend. It wasn't fair to hoard the worry for himself. He could see Jason was wrung out. Jason looked back at him steadily, clearly seeing what Ryan was trying to do.

"Don't, I'm fine," he said. "You need to be here when he wakes up, and for the record, Ryan, you need to fucking talk to him, sort this out. 'Cause you nearly killed him with your shit as effectively as this fucking earthquake. You're an idiot not to see what you have in Nathan." Ryan tried to reply, but stopped and nodded instead. "I'm gonna go find Laurie."

Ryan rested his head back down, aware his knees were starting to stiffen, but the ache was nowhere near as bad as the pain in his back.

As the noise of the chaos around him started to fade, he slipped into an exhausted unconsciousness, the top half of his body lying across Nathan's bed, finally able to give in, just for a few minutes.

CHAPTER 9

Phoenix Arizona, earlier that same day

Allison couldn't get comfortable. Her bump was a typical seven-month bump, but on her tiny frame, it looked like she was just going to give birth. She rubbed hands over her belly, making a mental note to have a frank discussion with Ryan's mom as soon as Ryan came clean with the whole *Oh shit, I'm going to be a dad and I'm not marrying the mother* thing. She needed some reassurances. Imagining six foot plus and built Ryan Ortiz, what size had he been when he was born? She swallowed, wondering if he'd been one of those ten-pound babies that made news headlines. She winced at the thought.

"You okay, babe?" Zack's voice was lost under the quilt. He had gotten very good at waking up when Allison was unsettled. She dropped a kiss on a small piece of available skin. He was pale where Ryan had been tanned, shorter where Ryan had been tall, soft where Ryan had been hard muscled, and he adored her. Best of all, he could handle the fact that she was pregnant with Ryan Ortiz's baby. He was, in every way, perfect.

They'd met at a magazine party almost two years ago, just at the time she and Ryan had started to fall apart.

He was a second editor. He was funny, smart, and he was a friend. They clicked, kept in contact by text, and he was a listening ear, discreet and supportive. He didn't comment when Ryan proposed. He just congratulated her and stepped back for a while to give the couple time to finally resolve the ongoing issues that they needed to handle. After they'd announced their engagement, three days was all it took for them to realize it was totally wrong.

It took another two days after that to realize that even being together as partners was wrong, and only one other day before Allison turned to her constant friend, depending on him to help her begin to pick up the pieces. He didn't approve of Ryan's visits, and he didn't disapprove. He was a friend, nothing more, and Allison could run her own life.

Between the Christmas flu and missing her pill, along with the visit from an emotionally upset Ryan, it was all a recipe for disaster, and a baby was made.

Zack wasn't with her when she told Ryan about the baby, but he held her after when she cried. He had become her support, and Ryan, despite his initial reservations, grew to learn that Zack was a good guy.

Zack and Allison had moved to Phoenix— it was where Zack had his house and Allison was happy there. It was taking that vital step towards being a couple, coming to terms with Allison being pregnant by Ryan and they were settled. Ryan had phoned, asked for someone to talk to, and arrived disheveled and half broken. Zack was immediately on guard. He informed her in no uncertain terms that he was going to fight Ryan for her if it came down to that. He loved her, and he wanted her to be his wife.

The whole other man bringing up her baby thing? Well, that was part of the conversation that Allison and Ryan had. Said conversation didn't stop until one in the morning, which ended up with Zack driving a determined Ryan to the airport to catch up with Nathan— to talk to Nathan. Zack told her that he'd spoken very little at first to Ryan, until finally it had to be said.

Allison was pacing when he returned, her face carefully blank, but happy at least to see him home. She grasped his hand, curling her small fingers into his and pulled him into the bedroom. They needed sleep.

And when, this morning, Zack asked her if she was okay, she meant it when she replied, yes. For the first time in months, she felt settled and happy.

"Nothing's up, Zack, just restless. He or she is playing football, m'gonna go and watch TV."

"Time is it?"

"Eight-thirty."

"D'ya need me to come with?"

"No, babe, sleep, I'll bring you some coffee in later."

She needed some peace now, some alone time, curling up on the sofa with orange juice and toast and turning on the TV. She focused in on what the ticker said along the bottom of the screen, reading every word as it slipped past in red and black on white.

The plate fell to the floor, and with a scream, a cry, a plea, she said two words, "No, Ryan," then another, "Zack!"

* * * *

"Ry?" Nathan's voice was so low, so quiet, hoarse and harsh. "Wha?" Nathan coughed with a groan and a grimace of pain as his chest was on fire.

"Ankle's broken," Ryan rasped as he jerked awake, his voice still croaky from the fire. "Ribs…your hip."

"Shit." *Is there anything that's okay?*

Nathan gripped hard on Ryan's hand. He wanted to say so much, wanted to thank him, to ask about Laurie, but all that came out was coughing, and Ryan pulled his hand free. Nathan shook his head, but Ryan was already levering himself to stand, his face pale and grimacing in pain. Nathan wanted to stop him. *Please don't go, talk to me.* But

Ryan's face was closed, his eyes half shut, and then he was trying to stand still and straight.

"Nathan?" The voice came from behind Ryan, and he felt Ryan move to one side. Jason? Jason is here, what the—

Nathan couldn't speak, he tried, but Jason stopped him. "Hey, dude, I was kinda worried."

Nathan quirked an eyebrow. "You were worried about me? I don't live in downtown LA." Jason smiled crookedly. He crossed to the bed, grasping Nathan's hand and squeezing reassuringly.

"Gotta get you outta here and on to a hospital, but I tell ya, it's chaos out there, Christ knows when it'll happen. They've pushed us as far back as they can, but we are getting too close to downtown LA evac, so they're clearing a new break line."

Nathan nodded, the information a whirl of words that he didn't hear, then frowned, looking past Jason for Ryan, but there was no sign of Ryan.

Jason shook his head and shrugged. "He's probably gone to find Laurie." Nathan shut his eyes against sudden pain in his chest. He knew Ryan had gone for a good reason but it didn't stop the pain that tightened, making breathing difficult.

* * * *

Ryan had passed through two makeshift tents, his eyes down, avoiding anyone's questions with a blank look and a shrug, until at last he came to area that he supposed could be designated the children's area. He circled until his searching gaze met Laurie's. Her eyes wide and frightened, she launched herself at him.

He scooped her up, and she resumed her position tucked into his neck. It felt good, and it felt safe. He turned to the harassed woman with the list as she looked at it, and then looked at him, clearly out of her depth. Still she stood in the doorway, determined to release the little girl to only someone on her list.

"Your name please."

"Ortiz, Ryan," he said, his voice burnt and husky.

"Do you have some ID, some..." Her voice tailed off as Ryan just stood in front of her, in a hospital-issue top, holding out his hands to indicate he had nothing. "I'm sorry, I just..."

"—back to the main area, my— friend is there." Ryan was struggling to get the words out.

She looked at him stricken, looking at one more child, one more small person without parents to look after her, and then to Ryan, someone to take responsibility. She looked over at the twenty or so children who sat around on the makeshift beds, every one of them alone, with no one. At least this little girl had someone, this Ryan.

"I need to check, I can't just let people, non-family— take the children." She watched as Ryan leaned back on the side of a bed, his posture clearly patient. He was willing to wait. "My team leader, he'll be back in a minute, to look at this."

"S'okay," Ryan said softly, his back tightening, the pain indescribable, and he tried to relax each muscle.

When the shouting started, Ryan simply held Laurie tight.

"Out, out, out, everyone, we need to get out... We need to get out. All those walking out…the fire…"

They held Ryan back, and they held the children back as they stood, screaming at the noise. Chaos erupted. He was pushed back, pushed away, over the ripped tarmac, pushed behind the new break line, the army swarming as they had to deal with people screaming for loved ones, staring in horror as the fire was darting and jumping down the hillside to the makeshift evac area. Ryan was desperately straining to get through, back to Nathan, to Jason, to warn them, his back pushed and jostled until fresh red blood ran down his scrubs, but it was no use. The panic was as good as a brick wall, impossible to force himself through.

He'd known that this was only a temporary evac area, an emergency, a stop gap, but surely they wouldn't have collected so many refugees in one area, medically attended so many injured people just for the fire to turn and burn them all to the ground.

He heard prayers shouted and screamed to the heavens, seeing people still walking, running, crawling from the area in danger to the front of the break line.

"Move back. Everyone move the fuck back. Let people through."

Nathan, Nathan...

"Will it jump? Oh my God, will the fire jump here?"

"Pray to God it doesn't."

Screams filled the air as the fire cracked like lightning and moved into the area, and in seconds, the inferno twisting and circling, wrapping the tents in flame, and each one fell, destroyed in seconds.

Ryan could feel the heat on his face as he fell to his knees, a silent scream locked in his mouth.

Nathan.

CHAPTER 10

Jason all but carried his friend out of the tent, never more grateful than he was right now for the extra height he had on Nathan. They were guided, herded, pushed out of the tent and down towards the new line break. Hundreds of people surrounded them, rushing and running to escape the approaching flames.

"I can't see him, J."

"He'll be with Laurie and the kids. Come on, man..." Jason looked at their path carefully, watching for the fire, as he tried to pull his friend to safety at the same time he worried about Ryan and the little girl.

People were shouting, screaming, begging for help around him, help to find loved ones, separated when they were processed for medical attention. Jason couldn't listen, couldn't hear. He concentrated one hundred percent of his effort in getting Nathan down past the new break the army had made.

Two hundred yards... They were moving so painfully slow. Why was no one running?

One hundred and fifty yards... The fire cracked and spit behind them.

One hundred yards. "Let them through, everyone just move back."

Fifty yards away, a man in uniform took Nathan's other arm, and between them, they dragged him past the uninjured.

Twenty yards… An eerie quiet settled as the flames swallowed the evac area,

Ten…

Five…

Jason slumped to the ground, Nathan half falling on him, breathlessly thanking the uniformed man who had risked his life to help people over the line. He gave them a small smile and then he plunged back into the smoke and flames to help more people. Jason memorized his face, the name on his uniform. *Kowolsky*. He would find him. After all this was finished, he would find him and thank him.

Medics scampered over fallen bodies, some lost to the trampling crowd, some just not fit to be moved. They shouted urgent instructions, and they quickly scanned Nathan, assessed his injuries non-life threatening, ordering that he move on.

"The fire is being held back. Get a fucking move on and move down as far as you can."

To the chaos that was the epicenter. They had no choice.

Jason helped Nathan to stand and began to slowly move down the hill, his eyes tracking the push of humanity, watching people reunite, watching people crying for others. He saw the children before he saw Ryan, a small group, sitting in a huddle with everyone walking round them.

"Ryan," Jason breathed softly, looking at the man who sat, huddled, his knees drawn up, Laurie clinging to his legs, his face a mask of grief. "Ryan!"

Ryan lifted his head, blinking, recognizing his name, but so lost in his grief, obviously not certain he was hearing right. He stumbled towards them over split ground, Laurie still clinging to him.

"Nathan." Ryan forced the words out and fell to his knees as gracefully as he could, and Jason helped Nathan put his head in Ryan's lap.

Nathan turned his head into Ryan's lap, grunting with the exertion of movement, and Ryan carded a hand through his short hair.

As they sat huddled close, Jason didn't say one thing that flickered through his mind. Nothing was as big as what they were facing. No petty paths in life, no worries, were as important as the struggle for life that was being won and lost around them.

"I'm gonna find out what's going on," Jason started, stopping only when Ryan grabbed at his hand

"Thank you," Ryan forced out, coughing.

Jason just shook his head imperceptibly. Nathan

was his friend. He didn't even stop to think of leaving the fire without him.

"I wanna know what happens next," he said simply.

Smoke and shadows swallowed him as he strode with purpose back up the hill to Army control. He hovered behind the small group of army personnel and fire fighters who were discussing what was happening.

"We can move the walking wounded down to level two, and join them to the evacuation from sector three," a fireman said simply.

"I can spare maybe three men to work through that."

"Level three is movement up from the City. We're just moving them from one danger—"

"I don't need commentary on the obvious; I need solutions."

"Level three? Jesus, what about aftershocks? What is the intel on—"

"We don't know; we have nothing."

"Start moving as many as we can down to level three."

"Sir."

Jeez, we are fucked.

He listened as best he could before forcing his way back through the milling crowd, back to Nathan and Ryan. This level three didn't sound too good, but shit, anything was better than sitting here with the fire frustrated and furious, hovering and spitting over the other side of the break, waiting for the right moment to cross, threatening and evil.

* * * *

Allison watched in horror as one of the CNN helicopters caught the last dying seconds of the evac area, lifting higher as the flames leaped into the sky. Open sobbing gave way to horror, her hands on her stomach, pain churning in her gut, the baby kicking inside her. She looked at Zack, eyes wide with fear. Ryan.

"It'll be fine. He'll have gotten out of that."

"You can't know that." Allison stood, the ache in her back intensifying. "How can you know that?"

"Allison."

"Stop saying it will be okay. Stop saying it!" She was shouting, the pains in her stomach acid hot.

Zack crossed to stand in front of her, touching her shoulder as she spun to push at him, hysteria rising in her "Ryan is dead. I know he is, and I sent him to Nathan. I did that."

"Stop, Allison, stop!" Zack shouted back at her. She knew it was perhaps the only way to break through her hysteria. She stopped as suddenly as she started, a hand unconsciously clutching at her swollen belly even as she fell sobbing into Zack's arms. He simply held her, whispering nothing into her ear but soft words to try and calm her down, even as she arched into him, a sudden cry on her lips.

"Zack, my baby, Zack."

It took the ambulance ten minutes to get to them, then another fifteen, and they were at the hospital.

"Are you her partner?" a young doctor asked Zack

Zack nodded. "Is she going to be okay?"

"She started going into labor. We've had to introduce measures to slow this down. Her notes say she's at twenty-eight, twenty-nine weeks, and that's far too soon for her to start labor. She'll need to stay here, monitored. If we can't stop this, we need to make a decision on pumping steroids for the baby's lungs."

"Oh my God."

The doctor just looked at Zack sympathetically.

"We'll do everything we can to make sure mother and baby stay well. She needs to rest and relax; she'll need you to help her do that."

CHAPTER 11

Jason stopped, resting a hand on Ryan's arm. "We need to get moving. They're moving us to a new evac area."

Ryan looked down at the barely conscious man, glancing at his hands twisted in Nathan's hair. "Meds?" he said softly.

"Yeah, they kind of knocked him out. His ankle is strapped, but we need to get him to a hospital or some sort of facility where they can X-ray and set the bones. I'll get Laurie, and we can move him down."

Jason stood, obviously scanning for Laurie. She sat not far away with a group of other children, all unnaturally quiet. He crossed to scoop her up, and Ryan watched him stop as other children stood to follow him. Ryan heard him trying to explain.

"I'm not…you can't…I can't…" But in the end he shrugged, and the group followed behind him back towards Ryan and Nathan.

Ryan shook Nathan. His green eyes opened slowly, blurred, and for a moment, it was almost as if he didn't recall what had happened. Then, just as suddenly, he seemed to remember, starting to struggle upright. Ryan helped him as best he could, trying not to wince as the newly opened wounds on his back stretched and pulled.

Jason stood in front of them, Laurie in his arms, helping Ryan to stand, supporting him as he swayed, seeing the fresh blood on the green scrubs, but not saying a word as Ryan stared at him, entreaty in his eyes.

Between them, Nathan stood, hobbling on one leg, waiting as Ryan threaded an arm under his. No one said anything. No words were needed, not even when the eight children started to follow Jason. Ryan just looked over at him, and Jason just shrugged again.

They stumbled and followed and made their way down, people urging them on, guiding them to the next evac area. Even with a broken ankle, Nathan was still considered walking wounded, but Ryan guessed he wouldn't want anyone's assistance anyway and just vowed to help him keep going. There were people hurt far worse than them, with burns, breaks, and lots of bloody injuries.

They had almost made it to the new area when another milder aftershock hit, nothing major, nothing that made anyone stop walking. Numb to the disaster around them, it distracted Ryan enough to not watch where his feet were going, and he stumbled on loose bricks, righting himself quickly, and seeing other bricks laying around him. In the spectral smoke, images started to form— a building, windows, more buildings, walls, shattered, heaved and thrown like a giant's playthings around the weary refugees.

Half of a sign lay on the ground —*spital*— and gave them enough to know where they were. Ryan was overcome with a strange kind of anger, a grief. What was the point? How were they going to receive medical attention in a hospital that was clearly destroyed? How was this place safer than the last? They might be away from the fire, but they had moved straight into earthquake central.

Three hundred people, four hundred, maybe even five, moved in a column onwards past the main hospital to a building hardly touched by the destruction around it. It was covered in the grays and browns of moving earth but seemed intact, safe, standing. He recalled in '94 after the Northridge earthquake, many hospitals were destroyed or rendered unusable. There was chaos in transferring patients, and he had watched a TV show focusing on it only a few weeks back. Something about the state legislature passing a law about California hospitals, making them ensure that their acute care units and emergency rooms were housed in earthquake-proof structures. Thank fuck for the law.

As they watched, a large army transport helicopter landed a distance away from them, and a group of people in scrubs started to move stretchers from the intact area to the waiting arms of army medical personnel. This was the evacuation point for the terminally injured, or those who needed special attention, and none of the newly arrived refugees walked to it, or watched it, or seemed to have any desperate hope to be on the waiting craft.

It seemed as if, as one, they knew that to be leaving on this flight, this particular evacuation flight, would mean they were close to death, and no one was ready enough to accept that fate. They huddled in small protective groups as army personnel started to move in amongst them, singling out the sick and the injured for medical attention.

It was an hour, maybe more, before it was Nathan's turn to be checked in the emergency area. He clutched at Ryan, insisting he was seen too, forcing his friend to turn round and expose the horror that was his shredded back. They were assigned a group and a doctor who was organized, quiet, and somber. Jason waited with Laurie and the children while Ryan and Nathan were hurried in through to the casualty department where doctors, surgeons, nurses and volunteers waited. They were the witnesses to untold horror. The light had dimmed in their eyes, and their faces showed their exhaustion from their continual work.

When would this day ever end?

Ryan lay on his front; numb, quiet, knowing Nathan was in the next cubicle. He had heard what the doctor told Nathan. His X-rays showed a fracture in his ankle, three broken ribs, some extensive soft tissue damage around a fracture in his hip, through his leg, and down to his knee.

The doctors hadn't been as forthcoming with him. X-rays weren't needed to reveal what his problem was. Where the concrete and glass had fallen on him, there were deep cuts, in three places to muscle, which explained the intense spasms of pain he was having. He had internal bruising and some damage that they were concerned would slow down the range of motion in his neck.

Where he'd tried to protect his head, his hands were now swollen and bruised beyond recognition. There were no suspected fractures, but a particularly bad cut appeared to have sliced into a tendon. He needed stitches and a multitude of tests for reaction time when the doctor expressed concerned about unusual swelling at the top of his spine where he'd received the worst hits.

The doctor said he was lucky the concrete hadn't been an inch or two lower as it may have damaged his spinal cord irreversibly. Ryan didn't say a thing, not even realizing for one minute that Nathan could hear as clear as day what the doctor said just as Ryan had heard Nathan's prognosis.

It wasn't until the doctor left, the nurse running to find more bandages and thread, that Nathan stood next to him, a crutch under his arm, his chest bare, his leg in plaster. Ryan couldn't turn over.

"Ryan." Nathan was whispering, unable to talk any louder, his throat still raw.

"Hey," Ryan said in an equally small voice.

"I heard what they said, Ryan. You wouldn't even have been injured if you... You shouldn't have put yourself in harm's way like that."

"Why?"

"You're hurt. Your spine... What if you'd received permanent damage?"

Ryan twisted his face to turn away from Nathan so he couldn't see his tears, "I'd do anything for you," he mumbled.

* * * *

Nathan couldn't hear, so he could either hobble round the other side of the bed, or actually get Ryan to look back at him.

"Please look at me, Ryan."

It took a few seconds, but he did at least turn. Nathan touched the tears on Ryan's face. "Are you in pain?" he asked softly.

Ryan shut his eyes. "No, yes... No, that isn't why."

"Can you tell me?"

"Have I...destroyed it all?"

"You mean us?" Nathan sighed, moving his thumb

to trace Ryan's lip and down to his bruised and swollen neck, a touch so gentle, even though Nathan knew they must have numbed Ryan's back. "No, Ryan. We need to talk, but when we need to talk... Jesus, it seems so small and pathetic compared to all of this."

Nathan bent down, wincing at the sharp insistent pain in his chest, his lips inches from Ryan's, a single tear tracking a path to the corner of his mouth. "I love you, Ryan. Doesn't matter what happens. I will always love you. I can't begin to understand what changed you, but I know you will tell me one day. Maybe you were scared, I don't know, but it will be fine when we talk. I promise I won't fly off in a huff, and you won't need to come into an earthquake zone looking for me."

He smiled slightly at the irony in his words, his own eyes wet, and then he dropped the smallest of kisses to the corner of Ryan's mouth, tasting the saltiness of his tears. Ryan tried to lift his head to chase the kiss, but his face reflected the magnitude of his pain. Nathan, however, sensing the need in Ryan, ran a collection of butterfly kisses over marked skin, feeling the muscle beneath, re-learning the taste.

"I'm sorry," Ryan tried to say, his voice so small. "I can explain, at least I can try. Allison—"

"Ryan, don't."

"No, let me finish. Allison is having a baby. Christmas, after I saw you with Jason, when I jumped to conclusions. Shit. I'm so sorry, it was once, I promise. In a few weeks, I'm going to be a dad."

Nathan was quiet for a little while, thirty seconds, a minute, no more.

"Okay," he finally said.

"Okay?"

"I'm not sure what else to say. Is Allison okay?"

"She's shine…fees shi…she fine."

"Shit Ryan, how could you… have you…" Nathan stopped. Why was Ryan's voice slurring and why the hell was Ryan choosing this moment to tell him when all around them things were falling apart? Was he going to reveal he was marrying Allison, playing a daddy role? Nathan's heart twisted. They were so close, but so far apart. Instead he said, "When is the baby due?"

"Cot…O…tober."

"Why didn't you tell me? Why couldn't you tell me? Ry?"

Ryan buried his face in his hands, groaning. He mumbled something, which Nathan couldn't hear.

"Seriously, Ryan, it doesn't matter. If you can't answer that now, we can cover… Ryan? Ryan?" Nathan suddenly felt fear clutch at him, Ryan was so still, so quiet.

Had he just fallen asleep or was he unconscious? It didn't look like he was moving at all. He had slurred his words. Was he even breathing?

"Can I get some help in here please?" Nathan hobbled to the curtain, "Help, my friend, Ryan, I don't think he's breathing. Can someone help him?"

What happened next became a part of the nightmare landscape as Nathan just watched helplessly.

"His airway's closed. Does he have any allergies?"

"I don't know…I don't know…"

"Stand back, get out of the way. Shit, he's coding…the neck, too much swelling. Who assessed this man? Next evac chopper is here. He's not gonna make it out if we don't… Scalpel… For God's sake, twenty milligrams…"

Jason, what's happening? Where are you? I need…

CHAPTER 12

It took two hours. They used paddles, shot electricity through his heart, cut into his throat, opened an airway... Pressure had built up at the base of his neck, edema, restricting air, starving him. It took two hours, and then he was evacuated, unconscious but alive, in the main evac helicopter that hovered ominously in the smoke-blackened sky for one precious second before wheeling away from them.

Jason was scared. Nathan had stopped talking, stopped asking questions, seemingly stopped breathing. He was so still.

"Nathan," he said softly, pulling the younger man back into the casualty area, not knowing what to say. He had Laurie wrapped in his arms as well, tears rolling down her face as they took Ryan away. Jason wanted to cry too.

They wouldn't let Nathan go with them, saying there was room for emergency evac patients only. It was at that point that Nathan went quiet. Ryan was being taken to a better-equipped casualty unit, another rung up the damn injury chain. It was five miles farther away, across the tip of the worst destruction. Fires were still burning, eating into the hills and other fires that would probably burn for days in the destruction of LA.

"I'm getting to that hospital," Nathan said. His first words for what must have been close to an hour.

"Nathan."

"I've decided. I want to be doing something positive, and that sure doesn't include me sitting around here with my thumb up my ass. The whole travel area is empty. It's just buildings, and I'm going—"

"No more running," Jason said. "We stay until there are empty spaces on the next evac out of here. I'm not arguing, damn it."

Nathan went to move, but Jason gripped him tight. He was an uninjured man, taller and heavier than the injured Nathan, and Nathan lost his fight. Grumbling and grimacing in pain, Nathan stopped moving, allowing his weight to shift, leaning against Jason.

Jason continued, trying to be as persuasive as possible. "We can help here, man. Wait until there is space on the next evac helicopter. Are you with me here?" Nathan stared at Jason, then back at the nine children sitting looking at him expectantly. "Nathan?"

"The kids," Nathan said suddenly. "We can process the kids, get some details, maybe look into reuniting them." He sounded a little unsure about whether that was a good plan or not. "I need to be doing something positive." Jason smiled, seeing light in Nathan's eyes.

"Yeah, that is a good idea, dude, a good idea."

* * * *

Zack hovered with intent outside the room. When the doctor arrived to check on Allison, she'd asked Zack to stay, but he felt uncomfortable, like maybe she was only asking because she felt she had to. He loved Allison, had loved Allison for a long time. It didn't matter that the baby she carried was another man's. It didn't matter one bit. He was determined to be the best husband and father he could be. He just wanted the chance.

He hoped to God that Ryan alive and safe. He wasn't sure what effect it would have if Allison lost Ryan, her best friend of so many years. Whatever he felt about Ryan and how he'd treated Allison, Zack thought Ryan did seem like a decent enough guy. He glanced over at the headlines on CNN, his heart heavy.

Thousands dead in LA quake, as many are trapped by forest fires still raging...

There was a strange sober feeling in the maternity ward, as much an extension of how he was feeling inside—empty, shocked, black. No one spoke about what was happening, no one cried or talked or commented. As one, the mothers-to-be sat in the relatives' area, some with partners, holding hands or offering small comforting gestures as they nurtured life inside them, watching life being destroyed in front of them.

It was an excruciatingly simple analogy, but one that rested in Zack's heart, an image he knew he would remember forever.

"Sir, Ms. Young has asked you to be present at the exam." Zack tore his eyes from the screen, focusing instead on a short nurse. He nodded, following her back to the room. The doctor waited patiently next to the woman Zack loved. Allison's eyes swam with tears. He immediately crossed to her other side, reaching out for her hand, careful of the cannula that was feeding drugs into her system.

"What, Ali? What's wrong? What have they said?" He looked anxiously between her and the doctor, who glanced briefly at notes.

"We have managed to stop the contractions, but Ms. Young needs to stay here for now. With many cases such as this, we can stop the premature labor and try and get some steroids in for the little one's lungs, but inevitably, this baby will be born early. We just need to make sure it's born as late as possible. Your little girl will need a lot of help, and the longer we keep her inside where it's safe the better.

"A girl? We're having a girl?"

The doctor glanced up, seemingly unconcerned that

she may have revealed a secret that needed to be kept.

Allison pulled Zack in for a small kiss, the tears swimming in her eyes starting to spill down her pale cheeks. "A girl, Zack, we're having a girl."

Zack's heart was lost there and then in that moment. They were having a girl.

Allison and Ryan and Zack were having a girl.

* * * *

Rachel was seven, kinda from LA she thought. Her mom was at the last evac area, injured. When they ran, she didn't know where her mom had been. She was very scared.

Alex, five, and his big brother Jack, eight, were separated in the rush from crashed cars. Their mom was at home in the suburbs. Their dad had been driving, and he'd passed them over to a rescuer just as an aftershock had thrown the ground around. Jack was convinced his dad was fine, and that any minute now, he would arrive to take him and Alex away. Well, that was what he was saying in front of a clearly worried Alex.

Cory and Peter, both nine, were neighbors, evacuees running together as their parents battled to save their houses. The last words from their parents had been, "Stay together, stay together…"

Patsy, nine, she was staying with an aunt in the same area as Cory and Peter. She'd been on a sleepover, painting nails and doing hair, and her aunt had gone back for the dog. She didn't know what had happened to her aunt, but her family was in Arizona.

The last three were all under five, so it was difficult to get details. Apart from names —Susie, Lisa and another Jack— Nathan had nothing.

And then Laurie, three, a Christmas baby, was concerned where Ryan had gone. He asked if her parents had been in the car with her, and she answered yes. When asked if she knew where they were, she said she didn't know.

Nathan started with Rachel. If her mom had been at the last evac, injured, then maybe she had been pulled down here. Maybe it could be a happy ending.

After a half an hour of searching and following the medical trail, he found her.

Still and cold in the makeshift morgue.

It was then, as he stood in the silent cold room, surrounded by white shrouded bodies, that it hit him just how real this was.

CHAPTER 13

When Ryan regained consciousness his first thoughts were of Nathan, but he couldn't move to see if he was there. He was immobile, lying on his front, his head full of cotton wool, his mouth so dry.

He woke with memories of a less than stellar admission of his impending fatherhood to the man he loved. Shit. Perhaps Nathan was sitting there, just out of view.

Nathan he attempted to say, but his throat wouldn't let him. He tried to understand what had happened to his throat. His hands travelled up to feel tubes about him. He didn't panic. *This is okay, I'm okay, we're both alive.* He'd speak to Nathan later, make him see everything was okay, and with that, he fell asleep.

* * * *

Jason came back from his travels around the hospital to report his latest findings, Rachel, Cory and Peter trailing him, to find Nathan sitting, his back against the wall, his legs in front of him, asleep. Laurie curled on his left side, and Susie and Lisa were on the other side, sharing his lap. The other kids were huddled in a heap of coats and blankets, all asleep like a pile of puppies. Nathan's breathing, even in sleep, was labored, and Jason winced—

his friend's ribs must hurt like a bitch.

He didn't know what Nathan had found out about Rachel's mom. But when Nathan had come back as white as a sheet and just slumped down the wall, drawing up his knees and wrapping his arms around them, he assumed it wasn't good news. Jason had painkillers in his hand, knew it was time for Nathan to take them, and trying not to disturb the children, he shook his friend's shoulder gently. His green eyes opened slowly, then he slightly startled even as Jason indicated *shhhh*. He handed him the tablets and then the water, and once he'd seen Nathan swallow them, he backed off, allowing his friend to relax into sleep again.

Laurie turned into Nathan's side, mumbling something in her sleep and twisting her hands into Nathan's shirt. She obviously felt safe. Jason looked around him at the children sleeping, knowing in his head that it must have been nearly twenty-four hours since the first earth tremor, but understanding in his heart, for Los Angeles, a lifetime had passed.

* * * *

The house phone rang. There was no reply, but the message was simple: If this is Ryan, or someone with news about Ryan, please contact Kathy, then there was a number, her cell.

Ryan didn't leave a message, just rang his sister's cell, his fingers clumsy on the small buttons. He was suddenly overcome with emotion as she answered, breathless and quick.

"Ryan?"

"Kathy." His voice was so raw, and his throat, where they had cut, so raspy, he could hardly make sound.

"Ohmygodohmygod Ryan, Ryan."

"Kathy..." Ryan didn't know what to say, and his voice filled with tears.

"Ryan, are you okay, where are you?"

"Hospital...throat." From his position lying on the hospital bed, he awkwardly handed the phone to the aide who stood next to him. She briefly explained the problem without making it sound dramatic, nodded, exchanged looks with Ryan, then as suddenly passed back the phone, a stricken look on her face. Ryan put it to his ear.

"...with you? Ryan, Ryan, man, is Nathan with you?" It was Adam; they were obviously playing pass the parcel with the phone and clearly Nathan's family and his had somehow met and stayed together through this. It made sense he supposed; only one state line and some eighty miles separated both families, and they had evidently pulled together in the face of the two men being lost to the fires.

"S'Okay." Ryan lied. He didn't know if evac was being organized, but he prayed it was, and that Nathan would be here soon. He looked at the aide, who breathed deeply and took the phone back, explaining that, no, Nathan wasn't at this facility, and yes, he was fine, and yes, he was being brought here soon. She handed the phone back.

"Adam," he rasped painfully

"Your mom," Adam said softly, then the noise of the phone being passed.

"Ryan, I know you can't talk, Ryan— oh my God, baby."

* * * *

Jason watched as Nathan opened his eyes and smiled down at the lap full of small children, all asleep and probably as warm as hot water bottles. Jason sat against the opposite wall, an answering small smile on his face. Nathan yawned and blinked.

"S'ten," Jason offered softly, knowing Nathan would ask. Twenty-seven hours since the quake.

"Sleep at all, dude?" Nathan asked, and Jason nodded. No sense in letting Nathan see he had hardly slept at all.

"Some. Was helping around a bit and some of the kids were kinda restless."

"You should have woken me, Jase, I coulda maybe helped."

"Nah, I handled it. Anyways, we are so outta here in two. Some new med staff came in, volunteers, and all the wounded have been triaged and moved. We're kinda some of the last left at this station."

"Where they moving us to?"

"They have a center, a children's center, they want us there. Well, they want the children there, and I'm staying with them." Jason didn't ask if Nathan was staying as well. He could see the conflict in his friend's eyes, the desperation to see Ryan, to make sure he was alright, warring against the need for the kids to maybe be reunited with their families. Finally, he saw a decision in the calm set of his friend's face.

"I'm coming with you," Nathan finally offered, closing his eyes briefly, a frown on his face. Jason sighed inwardly. It hurt him to see his friend like this, hurt him to see Nathan so desperate to make sure Ryan was mending but being unable to reach them, the two sites having no direct communication. Batteries had long since died in cells, reception was sporadic, and the only communication they did have, via the army, was restricted for emergencies only.

Jason had known Nathan for only a short time. They had met through the show and just fell into friendship as easy as breathing. To his mind, he'd never seen Nathan so conflicted. It had always seemed to Jason that Nathan saw events in black and white. He was so strong in his beliefs and his opinions— always so quiet unless he had something he needed to say, kinda shy, and desperate to keep to himself. Jason often pointed out that the Kentucky farm boy had sure chosen the wrong career if he wanted anonymity. Nathan had argued back that it wasn't anonymity he craved, just a small amount of personal space.

And now, looking over as Nathan began one by one to wake up the children with quiet words and hugs, words of reassurance slipping from his tongue, Jason had his first real look at the desperation in his friend's face whenever Ryan's name was spoken. Every child asked where Ryan was. Jason sighed and made to stand, helping to peel off each sleepy child, finally helping a sleep-stiffened Nathan, his leg straight in front of him to protect his ankle, to his feet.

"Think I may need some more," Nathan wheezed, his free hand moving to his chest, "pain killers." He was breathing steadily, but his face was pale, and a sheen of sweat glistened on his skin.

"I'll grab some. Can you stand okay?"

"Standing...not a problem...breathing more so," and then Nathan smiled, a wry smile, a sarcastic Nathan-smile, and it made Jason feel less deathly worried and more just normally worried.

"Come on, man, let's go get these kids back where they belong and go find Ryan, yeah?"

"Yeah."

They all clambered aboard the next transport through the smoke hanging the air and the dust clogging their mouths and noses. Each child was passed up carefully from Jason to Nathan and, assisted by crew, strapped into place. Jason jumped up and sat next to Laurie, holding her hand and whispering something to her as the rotors started and they waited for the speed of them to pick up.

The sudden stomach-falling feeling of lifting from the ground made Nathan's head spin, and he felt several sets of small hands clutch at his army issue jacket. Sooner than he wanted, they were airborne. The men had been warned they would be taken above the low level smoke, that they would cross the top edge of LA, and that they would see things that maybe the kids should be kept from seeing. They tried.

The climb through the spinning, wheeling smoke was disorientating and brutal. It sent shivers down Jason's spine, like the climb to the top of a roller coaster before the fall. He didn't want to see LA destroyed. Not his city. He needed to see, but he didn't want to.

At first it was difficult to make out. The ground below was hidden by the low-hanging pall of smoke and a large debris field, but LA was tall. LA had buildings that kissed the sky in their grace and beauty, or it once had. Now they had mostly gone. Some remained, the glass gone, tilted, slanted, their backs broken, as if a small breath would topple them to the hidden floor below. Blinds hung out of eyeless frames, and desks, chairs, and jumbled furniture were only briefly seen as the chopper climbed higher, escaping the height of the tallest remaining buildings.

An insistent glow of orange travelled the tallest skyscrapers, fires burning unceasingly inside, fuelled by the normal parts of office life. Surely these buildings would have been virtually empty so early in the morning. Surely hardly anyone had died. The people who commuted would have still been at home, and they wouldn't have been at desks, trapped… Would they?

Jason realized he couldn't identify much of what was left, couldn't make out the skyline from the ruins below, and part of him wished he had a camera to capture the stark destruction, to understand where the LA he knew had gone. He looked over at Nathan, seeing tears in his friend's eyes, wishing he could cry himself, wishing he had something in him that would snap and let out the emotion that was eating away inside of him.

He couldn't indulge in his own fears and sorrow, not in front of the kids. He recognized Nathan's protective way of dealing with things had taken over, shutting him down, and his usual safety valve to release the tension —Ryan— was nowhere near him. Nathan had said in their alcohol fuelled talk a few days before the quake that he could always rely on Ryan to talk him out of his isolated coping mechanism, prank him out of it, joke with him, make him laugh, kiss him... Jason wanted to help in the same way, but it was impossible.

Nathan was clearly desperate for information on Ryan, frantic to see him. Jason hoped they would find Ryan whole and awake, not the white-bandaged, still body they'd flown away the night before.

Jason turned away from Nathan, because he couldn't bear to see the tears on his friend's face. Instead he looked over the vista that was a burning, destroyed LA. He felt empty.

CHAPTER 14

When they arrived at the new area, Nathan sat down tiredly. Jason took care of booking the children into the children's center, but Nathan kept Laurie on his lap. She was the very last to be processed. Nathan didn't want to let her go, and Ryan wouldn't want him too.

"Sir, Mr. Richardson, we just need to process this little one now."

"I know..." He paused. "Her name is Laurie, Laurie Allen, and she's three. We found her up by Dryden, in the hills, in a car."

"Can you describe the car, sir? Or any other details?"

"I didn't... My partner, Ryan, Ryan Ortiz..."

"Can you spell that for me, sir?"

Jason took over, spelling and giving as many of Ryan's details as he could. Nathan took advantage of the time, pulling Laurie in for one last hug before standing and passing her over to the kindly woman taking the details.

"We can check back." Nathan knew he wanted to see if Laurie was happy, if she had been reunited with someone...anyone.

"You can, sir, you can."

Nathan and Jason watched as the last of their babies

were taken through the security doors. They had seen inside, knew it was a better environment than following around two tired men, but still, to see Laurie waving over the woman's shoulder was not good, not good at all.

"Nathan, let's go find Ryan."

* * * *

Doctors and nurses fussed around him. "Ryan Ortiz, presented with blah blah blah..."

Ryan sighed inwardly. All he really heard when they were discussing him were long words that meant, bottom line, they had to cut his throat. That translated in his head to blah blah blah. *Lovely.*

They asked him to roll on his front again. Deft fingers lifted his bandage and checked his back. The pain shooting into his shoulder made him wince. The owner of the hands apologized, and he tried to shake his head, he really did, but jeez, the top of his spine was on the really bad side of painful.

They left him alone after injecting something into his drip, probably some kind of sedative as he hadn't really slept properly. They didn't seem to think unconsciousness counted. He felt as if he was drifting, but he was able to focus on the fact that Nathan wasn't here with him and that

Jason and Laurie were still somewhere out there. God knows when he'd be able to find anything out about his friends.

He tried really hard not to focus on Nathan, tried not to worry, but it was so damn difficult. However hard he tried, his last thoughts, as always, were of Nathan. Wondering where he was, if he was okay, if he was wondering the same thing about Ryan or whether he might be feeling he'd had a lucky escape.

I love you, Ryan whispered in his head, and let the stealthy warmth pull him into sleep.

* * * *

Nathan watched Ryan fall into sleep from the side of the curtain. He'd been warned by the nurse not to interrupt, as according to her the patient hadn't slept since he was brought in. He wanted to talk, to make Ryan see he was here, but instead he waited until the mask of deep sleep fell over Ryan's face and then he moved in, carrying a chair and slumping into it next to the bed.

His eyes traced the injuries on Ryan's back. The nurse explained some of them had been left uncovered as opposed to bandaged, as they watched hourly for infection. Antibiotics were being pumped into him. They were concerned about the neck injury, because the edema had been a shock, the swelling that closed his throat sudden and frightening to Ryan. Nathan couldn't even begin to contemplate the fear.

Suddenly uncomfortable in his own skin, he stood, shaking, desperate for touch, desperate to give comfort. Leaning over Ryan, his lips inches away from Nathan's face that was turned to one side, so perfect and still in sleep, he lowered his lips, touching a kiss to cool clean skin, his lips touching chin and cheek and then into the tangle of hair laying across his forehead. He re-learned the muscles in Ryan's strong shoulders, every muscle that wasn't bandaged, and every delicate bone that moved under the skin.

His fingers trailed after his kisses, tears falling unbidden from his eyes. The kisses he pressed to Ryan's skin were promises, pleas, prayers, and they patterned to his long smooth neck, the scar from the emergency surgery, the swelling, the faint veins, the pulse fluttering in a rhythm that Nathan could taste against his tongue.

He pulled back slightly, the tears pushed from a grief so deep he could feel it inside him, as gently he traced each defined muscle and injury on Ryan's strong back. That he had come for him, put himself in harm's way, didn't leave him, and had almost died to help him proved something. He knew Ryan loved him. How could he not love him back? Have ever doubted?

He trailed his fingers from the base of Ryan's spine, kissing and cataloguing each injury, the scarring and cuts crisscrossing his smooth skin, the field stitches stark and pulling pale torn skin together in a parody of art. Tears still fell silently, and Nathan absently brushed them into Ryan's skin, just learning and touching, happy and content to follow each scar and remember each act that put them there.

It was after a few minutes that Nathan sensed Ryan was waking. He felt faint tremors moving in him, a tightening of skin, a subtle movement of muscles, and then Ryan raised his head, looking directly into Nathan's eyes staring back at him, his pupils wide. Nathan placed a finger carefully of Ryan's dry lips, "Shhhhh."

Nathan wanted to say so much, wanted to shout at Ryan for throwing himself in harm's way, wanted to hug him until he couldn't breathe, wanted to taste him, love him... He didn't know where to start. How could he say all this, do all this?

Gently, Nathan moved back, face to face with Ryan, kissing him gently, once, twice, simple soft promises, before moving back to sit in the seat, a hand still touching Ryan's arm.

"Go back to sleep. I'll be here when you wake up."

* * * *

Flick.

...three days since what has been described as the worst natural disaster ever to hit the mainland United States—

Flick.

Now standing at just over six thousand dead, with what is thought to be in the region of one hundred times that homeless, and now we cross to Briony at—

Flick.

...heartbreaking thing is the children. Thousands of children have been split from parents in the frantic rush to escape from the—

Click.

Nathan threw the control down on Ryan's bed in disgust, the sleeping man not even moving at the sudden movement on his covers. The news coverage didn't change. It hadn't changed in the last hour, and it probably wouldn't change in the next week. People would be eating and breathing the disaster in LA for quite a while; they had no choice.

When Nathan had spoken to Adam and to the Ortiz family, they had said CNN kept them in contact with what was happening, seeing how rescue was being co-ordinated, seeing survivor stories. But all Nathan could see was the chaos around him, people still being airlifted in, pulled from the rubble, knowing they would perhaps be some of the last people to be pulled out alive.

CNN put the dead at six thousand, but the quake had hit the Latin areas heavily, and no one really had a handle on population there. The news seemed to focus on the fact that so many lived because the quake happened before the morning rush to work, giving hope where Nathan failed to see much now. Too many body bags, too much death, too many children.

It didn't help that he'd had an incredibly difficult conversation with Zack. No one had told Allison anything; Zack had ended up phoning Ryan's mom and kept in contact that way. Nathan hadn't told Ryan's mom about the baby, because he knew Ryan hadn't told them yet. Allison had gone into early labor. Could they get Ryan back? She needed him, she needed to see him… His baby was arriving soon, and there were complications. They talked about survival rates… How much more could Ryan take?

Nathan didn't say a word. He didn't tell Ryan; he just spoke to the doctor who pushed up discharge as much as he could, primed Nathan with meds, and wished them Godspeed. This time tomorrow they would be on the way out of LA and east to Phoenix. He just didn't want to be the one that told Ryan his baby might be dying.

"I'm gonna go see Laurie," he announced to his unconscious friend, snagging his jacket and leaving the room. He was still wearing his emergency scrubs, his jeans cut off when the blood and the gashes and the broken ankle had demanded it. So many people wondered around the same, in mismatched, ill-fitting clothes. Nathan wondered where they would find clothes to fit six-four Ryan when he was booked out tomorrow.

Ryan still couldn't talk properly. They had exchanged very few words when he was conscious. It was mostly just Ryan listening to the bits and pieces of news that Nathan managed to pick up on his travels in and around the hospital.

Nathan was worried about him more than he let on. His back was still so scarred, and some of the marks were so deep and red, and he seemed low, not just in pain, but low like the spark had been snuffed out of his expressive brown eyes. They hadn't talked yet, but Nathan had been there for him, telling him he loved him, kissing him gently to sleep.

He just knew Ryan's memories wouldn't be that he had saved Nathan, saved Laurie… The man he had to leave in the car —David Jackson— would haunt him, dragging him down, and Nathan didn't know what to say. Nathan was the one that had made Ryan go back, look into that man's eyes and tell him they were sending help, even as the fire crept towards him. It was Nathan that had made Ryan do that, and the guilt building inside him was like an acid.

He'd spoken to Ryan's family on his behalf, stuff Ryan tried to get him to say, making the rest of it up and saying what he thought they would want to hear. His own family had been easier. He'd just told them he was good. He didn't whitewash the whole trapped-under-a-beam business, but he did at least give it the Hollywood ending, something that was in short supply around here at the moment.

Stepping out into the California sun, he was surprised to see that the heavy smoke had started to dissipate. The fires in the hills had been brought under control, and the fires in LA were being left to burn themselves out. Some were so deep in rubble they couldn't be reached. He stopped briefly at the outside wall where a collection of missing person photos was starting to build. He had started to count the hours he was here by the size of the groupings, reading some of the details, wondering if any of these people would be found.

It was only a short walk to the children's center, short enough to make it easy on his ankle, long enough to actually get some air, smoke filled or not. They knew him at the front desk. He signed in. He knew where he was going, and before he knew it, he was at the dorm that held, at last count in this dorm alone, twenty-two children under the age of four. The guard who sat and watched and the group of nurses who huddled around various groups kept on doing what they were doing. No one stopped Nathan, and he spotted Laurie way before she spotted him. A woman was cuddling her, her back to him, hunched protectively around Laurie.

"Nathan," Laurie said happily, and in a flurry of movement, the woman stood, sweeping Laurie on to her hips and looking startled.

"Hey, Laurie Lee," Nathan smiled, "you okay, sweetie?" Laurie just grinned back, but she didn't hold her arms out for her usual hug, instead gripping tight to the lady.

"Mr. Richardson?" The women held out her hand.

Nathan shook it even as he acknowledged the name with the usual, "Nathan." He was still bemused, but assumed she was some sort of volunteer. She just stared at him, her eyes red, from smoke or crying he couldn't tell.

"I only just made it up here. I've been trying to find… I don't know what to say to you… your friend. They told me…" She stopped, her eyes filling with tears. "I'm Laurie's mom. Laurie was visiting her dad and his wife… I want to thank you, I want to thank you for my daughter... And I don't know how." She burst into tears, and Laurie snuggled in as her mom pulled her tight.

That was wonderful. It was what he and Ryan wanted, for Laurie to have family, for her not be on her own, but he didn't know what to say, how to vocalize just how happy he was. "You don't need to thank us," he said softly, because really she didn't, because when it came down to it, it was Laurie that had kept both him and Nathan going.

"I do... What you did, you and your friend, Ryan... Laurie told me, they told me here, that you pulled her from the car, that you carried her down... I don't know how I can ever repay you."

"You don't ever need to, but there is... Can you just do one thing for me?"

CHAPTER 15

Ryan was pissy and tired. Nathan had pulled him out of sleep and was helping him to sit up, and he hurt, damn it. He hurt from the base of his spine to the tip of his head, and why? 'Cus someone wanted to meet them, probably some fan who recognized his name and wanted a photo. Well, it wasn't as if he was in top form. All he wanted to do was—

"Ryan!" Laurie's voice.

Ryan's heart lifted, and he held out his hands as the three-year-old scrambled up on his bed and threw little arms around his neck

"Laurie, babe, you okay, sweetie?"

"S'momma," she mumbled into his neck as Ryan lifted his eyes and met dark brown eyes so similar to Laurie's that he knew in a heartbeat who the woman was.

"Your momma, darlin'?" he said softly, trying not to wince as she pulled on the back of his neck tightly.

"Uh huh."

He pulled her in for a hug, kind of knowing inside this might be the last time he got to do that. He owed this small child so much. She was the light in the dark, the one that kept him going when he could have stopped, and all those other clichés that were clutching at his heart right about now. The tears started way down inside, twisting his stomach. A skipped heartbeat, and the agony of failure and seeing the enormous vista of destruction about them flared deep inside. He couldn't let the tears out. He had to be happy; he *was* happy, happy to hand Laurie back with a squeeze and a kiss to her mom. Her mom, who was saying something, words that refused to filter through the noise buzzing in his head. *Thank you.... Sorry... Forget.*

He saw Nathan write something down and smiled somehow. He heard Nathan making medical excuses for him and heard him make promises before helping Laurie and her mom out of the room. He was only gone a while, but Ryan stayed sitting up. He needed to say something to Nathan when he came back. He wasn't sure what, but something to somehow explain the situation and what was in his head, starting with apologies and reasons.

Nathan came back into the room, crossing immediately to Ryan, and sitting down to face him, drawing one leg up and leaning in worried.

"You okay, Ryan?"

"I...yeah... I'm cool," he whispered, saving his voice.

"I was blown away when her mom said who she was and—"

"Sorry, Nathan, sorry," Ryan interrupted,

swallowing, then grimacing in pain. "I didn't tell you about the baby… treated you like shit… used you… didn't let you in… That isn't me…it's not me."

"Ryan, I know, I know it wasn't you, but it was too late. I'd already…" He paused, watching as the light in Ryan's expressive hazel eyes dimmed. He sighed. "It didn't matter, Ryan, not really, not underneath, 'cus I'd already decided it wasn't the real you. You were controlling and jealous, yeah, but nervous, anxious, and sad as well. I just wanted my Ryan back, the Ryan that made me feel, the Ryan I fell in love with, and I just didn't know how to find the real you."

They fell silent, Ryan breathing heavily, Nathan resting his forehead on Ryan's, breathing in synch, waiting.

"…go home," Ryan whispered.

"We have stuff we need to do, Ryan. Family. Then I promise you, I promise we'll go home."

* * * *

It came to Nathan at four in the morning as he tossed and turned in pain on the camp bed on Ryan's floor, his ribs protesting at every movement.

He couldn't sleep, and took to his usual early morning wander around the hospital, tracking down the nurses that babied him with coffee and trying to locate the newly disappeared Jason. Jason who'd spent an awful lot of time in the pediatric area, just helping and supporting and making himself quite the name as being Mr. Jason, the funny one.

He finally located him, lying on his back and snoring softly outside the nurses' area. Nathan shook him gently, and he mumbled in his sleep before turning over and seeing who was waking him. Realization hit him suddenly, and he sat bolt upright, anxiety on his face.

"Ryan?" he said urgently

"Nah, sorry, he's cool, sorry, I didn't mean to scare you."

Jason relaxed immediately. "Wassup?"

"We're gonna try making it out tomorrow. We need to get to Phoenix."

"And you need to get to Phoenix because?"

Nathan sighed. There wasn't really an easy way to explain this without the big reveal. So, like ripping a Band-Aid off of skin, he just blurted it out.

"Allison is pregnant, and she's gone into premature labor. They're not so sure that the baby is gonna make it. It's Ryan's baby, dude, and Ryan doesn't know the baby is in danger, but if he has any chance to say goodbye, or make his peace or whatever, we need to take it." Nathan shrugged and took a breath.

To his credit, Jason didn't flinch and didn't ask any awkward questions. He just reached into his dark-stained jeans and pulled out keys, pulling one off the ring and handing it to Nathan.

"I don't know if it's still there, man, but if you can get to my parents' ranch then my SUV is garaged there." The ranch was what Jason called his parents' horse-breeding farm. Nathan had been there a couple of times. It was way out of LA, past the hills.

"I don't know what to say. Thanks."

"No thanks, Nathan, just get him there in time, yeah? Try and make sense of it all."

They hugged briefly, and then with a last smile, they separated.

"Later," Jason said as Nathan walked out...*later.*

* * * *

When they managed to get to the city limits, it was already early evening, and the regime of painkillers was due again. Ryan looked really ill, and Nathan doubted he looked much better. They had passed through checks and roadblocks, following the small trickle of people that were heading out of the city. They hitched a lift on a convoy, and

Nathan had shamelessly begged to use the army communications system and had managed to get in touch with Adam. He was relieved that he had managed to pass on messages to both families. It was another tick in the plus column, and Nathan could see Ryan unwind inch by inch as they moved across the county.

It was late evening when they arrived at Jason's family's house. It lay in total darkness, empty. No horses remained. The fire hadn't gone back that far, but they had obviously evacuated. The SUV was where Jason had said, covered and locked.

Ryan leaned against it. "Need to stop," he said, forcing out the words.

"We can't. We need to keep moving."

"No rush… safe. Stop…one night."

"We need to go to Phoenix to see Allison. She needs to see you are okay."

"'morrow."

"No, come on, get in." Gently he helped Ryan onto the back seat, folding his jacket as a pillow and placing a blanket from the back of the seat over his already dozing friend. Quietly he climbed into the front, pushing away exhaustion, focusing on where he was going, visualizing Phoenix from LA. *Five hours, six, a break, maybe seven.* Either way, Nathan planned to have Ryan at the hospital by daybreak.

CHAPTER 16

Allison was crying quietly as the pediatrician explained the situation. They had managed to push it to twenty-nine weeks according to scans, eleven weeks early, but they couldn't hold off any longer. She heard their words over and over in her head: *Thirty two percent chance of survival...lungs will be weak...we'll try our hardest.*

Zack had looked at her, just looked as they explained the dates to her. He was with Allison now; he had to refocus her away from Ryan for her own good, away from the pain she was in, had to get her to realize so much didn't matter, dates or not, sleeping with her ex once or twice or thirty times. What mattered was now.

She curled up in pain, the contractions closer and closer as he sat there, and he waited before taking her hand.

"Ali, doing great, I love you Ali, it's all fine, s'gonna be okay."

She gripped his hand, and Zack looked at the people that stood round the bed. The emergency physician, the surgeon, the anesthesiologist, then back to stare into Allison's intense eyes, feeling the love as a contraction pulled her from inside, and she arched forward into Zack's shoulder.

"S'gonna be okay, Ali, okay."

* * * *

"We're here, Ryan, can you wake up? You need to wake up." Nathan touched Ryan's shoulder. He seemed warm to the touch, and Nathan guessed they were in as good as place as any if Ryan was running a fever. He watched as Ryan forced open his eyes, then helped him to sit and then finally climb out of the SUV. Ryan blinked as he looked around, realizing he wasn't at Zack's house but at a hospital.

"Shit, Nathan, seriously no, no 'spital," he managed to choke out, coughing, massaging his throat as he coughed.

"We need to go in."

"No… to sleep." Ryan stubbornly pulled back.

"Ryan, we need to go in." He paused, not quite sure how to phrase it, looking up at the dawn sky for inspiration. When it came down to it, there really was no other way to say it. "Allison's in there, Ryan. There's been a problem with the baby." He watched as Ryan's eyes widened, flicking uncertainly between Nathan and the automatic doors to reception.

"'s bad?" Ryan asked quietly, but all Nathan could do was shrug and frown.

"They just told me to get you here. I don't know, not really." He locked the car and moved to the doors, and then he waited, watching Ryan stop, not moving towards the entrance doors with a look of pure fear on his face. He saw other emotions passing in quick succession, anger, sadness, resignation, hopelessness. He'd forgotten just how expressive his Ryan's face was. He finally saw focus, and watched as, drawing himself to his full height, Ryan crossed to the doors to stand next to him.

"S'go," Ryan said softly, and then Nathan took over, moving them to the reception.

"We're here for Allison Young. Ryan Ortiz, Nathan Richardson." He didn't even want to think what they looked like. Ryan swathed in bandages, pale, his hair long and straggly, looking gaunt and exhausted. Nathan only marginally better, the cast on his ankle, both in scrubs.

To her credit, the receptionist said nothing, just directed them to the maternity ward.

"…plans with her," Ryan choked out in the elevator to the fourth floor.

Nathan was getting very good at Ryan speak. "You had plans to be with her? What? When she had the baby?" Ryan nodded, but that didn't surprise Nathan. He knew, even though the Ryan-Allison relationship was no more that Ryan would want to be there when his baby made its entrance. "That's cool, Ryan. You'll make a great dad."

"Sorry." He gripped at Nathan's arm, his eyes pleading, seeming to say *Are we gonna be all right? Is this gonna be okay with you?*

"It's all cool, Ryan, can't wait to meet Ortiz Junior." And he gently placed a hand over Ryan's as the elevator door opened and they took a step into the hallway.

"Ryan!"

The two men turned. Ryan paled further at Zack's face, twisted in concern, and they walked towards one another, Ryan going as fast as he could.

"Shit man, it's good to see you. Allison went into premature labor. Your daughter…she's here. Allison is doing poorly; they have her on a drip, and she's asleep. She had quite a bit of bleeding. The baby's name is Millie. Ryan, come see."

Zack pulled at Ryan's arm, only releasing it at the wince, then guided him down the corridor to a series of marked doors, pushing into one marked NICU. He then stopped at a window, looking in at frightening machinery, a mass of wires and plastic and color, and in the midst of it, so tiny she could fit in Ryan's hand, his daughter, Millie.

"Okay?"

Nathan looked at Ryan. There was so much emotion in that single word. Zack seemed to know exactly what

Ryan was asking.

"They are looking after her. She's twenty-nine weeks, Ryan, very small. They are worried about her lungs, but they managed to hold off labor long enough to pump in some steroids, and, I dunno, man, but she looks like a fighter. They won't let us in, none of us except Allison, not until the first forty-eight hours have passed."

"Can Ryan speak to a doctor? See Allison?" Nathan asked even as he knew Ryan wanted to ask the same thing. Ryan looked at Nathan gratefully.

Zack looked around quickly. "I'll find the doc. Allison's in room forty-five. She's allowed visitors, but I'm not convinced she's gonna be waking any time soon. The last few days have hit her really hard."

"What..." *What caused it? Why did the labor come on so quickly?* Zack clearly knew what he was trying to ask.

"Shock I think, Ryan, shock at what was happening in LA, at her feeling she sent you to your possible death, a combination of these. No one's fault, except nature's."

Ryan unconsciously leaned into Nathan for support.

"Come on, Ryan," Nathan encouraged, "let's go see Allison, then get some more information on Millie. Yes?" Ryan just nodded. *Good. Positive action is always good.* They walked down the corridor away from NICU. Ryan looked dazed until they reached room forty-five. The door was shut. Nathan knocked, but there was no answer, so there were no doctors inside, probably just one sleeping Allison. Ryan pushed the door open, and Nathan stood back. It wasn't his time to be with Ryan. This was Ryan and Allison's time.

"I'll be outside. I'm gonna go find Zack and get some coffee, okay?"

* * * *

Ryan closed the door behind him, turning to look at the diminutive form of Allison, still and very pale against the white sheets. Sighing, he positioned himself in a chair next to her, willing her to wake up, wanting to see her eyes. He sat for a long time. How long he didn't know, but long enough for Nathan to bring him pain meds and water and also much wished for coffee.

Nathan brought him food, breakfast he supposed, but his stomach churned at the coffee which he only drank for the much needed caffeine, so there was no chance of keeping down the food. He had also dragged in a more comfortable high-backed leather chair, each time leaving with a soft kiss and words of encouragement.

Ryan leaned his head back in the chair, his throat scars tight and itchy, his head pounding with a fierce headache, his back arched to keep the scarred sore areas from touching the chair. The doctors had been in to check on Allison. Apparently they'd had to deal with some internal bleeding, hence the anesthetic, but they didn't go in to any more details, probably sensing that Ryan was already on overload.

Zack had spent some time in here as well, but he had sat hunched up on the old chair on the other side of Allison, grasping her hand. He spoke some, in small details, about her worries, her fears, the baby, the shock of it all. He spoke of loving her and promising to do the best for Allison and Millie. He promised the baby would carry Ryan's name, and then subsided into a silence so sudden it brought Ryan out of his daze to look over, concerned. Zack had a wry smile on his face. He probably realized that he'd been talking Ryan's ear off. Ryan just smiled back and nodded. He liked Zack.

Zack had been gone five minutes when she woke up. "Ryan?"

Ryan immediately looked over at Allison, reaching for a hand and squeezing it gently, giving her a smile. She looked stricken.

"She's fine," Ryan forced out immediately, and she relaxed.

"So sorry, Ryan, I'm so sorry I sent you, and then the baby."

"No —thank you— both." *Thank you for my beautiful daughter, thank you for making me see sense with Nathan, thank you.*

* * * *

Nathan stood at the NICU window, just watching the calm and ordered way that the staff went from each incubator to another, looking after their tiny charges. They held the miracle of life in their care, and he was in awe. Zack materialized at his side, coffee in hand.

"I'm gonna go back in to Allison, but thought I'd maybe catch up with you before I did," he said, handing Nathan a black coffee and half leaning against the glass. "Ryan is just sitting there watching and listening to me ramble on," he added, sipping at the hot liquid and wincing at the heat.

"His throat." Nathan touched his own throat, remembering the scars, remembering almost losing Ryan. "It's quite badly damaged. It needs time to heal, otherwise I'm telling you that there wouldn't be a chance in hell of you getting a word in edgewise."

"Yeah, I know, I mean I kinda got to know him a bit over the last few months. I wonder if Millie will take after him." He looked back into NICU, focusing on the little baby, a frown on his face. Nathan felt concern shoot through him.

"Are you worried that she will?" he asked. Zack looked up, immediately horrified.

"God, no, I don't care who she takes after. But I mean, having a six-four daughter when Allison is like five nothing and I'm only five ten, shit, can you imagine?"

"You're in for the long haul then?" Nathan asked curiously.

"Putting it that way makes it sound like I have to make a decision. There is no decision. I love Allison and I am going to ask her to marry me. I-I spoke to Ryan about it, the night he left for LA, for you. He," Zack paused, "he seemed cool with it."

Nathan wanted to say something useful, something supportive, like maybe he could understand how Ryan would be cool with this, but his heart wouldn't let him, and instead he offered a small —and what he hoped came across as understanding— smile. He'd forever be the model with the perfect smile, but it usually worked for him.

And it seemed to work with Zack. He smiled back then wandered off down the corridor, leaving Nathan still standing watching Millie, lost in his own thoughts. When it came down to it, how was Ryan going to face giving this up? How could he be *cool* with Zack bringing up his baby, being with his girl? How could he decide to be with Nathan when last Christmas he had slept with Allison?

A soft touch on his arm and the object of his thoughts was there, pale and exhausted. Nathan pulled him close, and for a few minutes, they looked in at baby Ortiz-Young before Ryan started to try and talk.

"Shower…bed." He held out a hand, a credit card in Zack's name, and a cell phone, probably also Zack's. A room, a shower, somewhere, anywhere, sleep.

"Sounds good, Ryan, let's go." And the two walked out of the hospital, Nathan holding Ryan's hand, tugging him gently to the SUV and helping him in.

They booked into the first clean-looking motel they found, let the hospital know where they were, and then phoned home. Nathan did the talking for Ryan, who tried to sign what he wanted to say. He then took a pad of hotel paper and a pencil and wrote one sentence. *I need to tell them about Millie.*

"Hang on a sec, Mrs. O, Ryan has written something down." He covered the cell phone in his other hand. "Dude," he stared into hazel eyes that pleaded with Nathan to help him, "are you sure?" Ryan nodded, and Nathan breathed deeply. "Hi, I er, Ryan has asked me to tell you why we have stopped in Phoenix, why we haven't flown home. Allison is —was— pregnant. She had the baby prematurely. She's in Phoenix, at Memorial, and the baby was born at twenty-nine weeks. Her name is Millie, and she's fine. Very small, but very beautiful."

He paused as he listened to questions and comments on the other end, his face carefully blank as he continued to hold Ryan's tear-filled gaze. "Ryan wanted to tell you, wanted you to know, the baby is his. She's your granddaughter."

CHAPTER 17

Zack had settled himself in for another night of watching and waiting, more coffee in his hand and a newspaper on the table next to him. Allison was still awake, groggy, but had managed to spend time with Millie, touching her baby's skin through the hole in the incubator, a tiny hand clutching at her finger, a spark of hope inside her that she hadn't killed her baby, that Millie would be fine.

She looked over at a quiet and content Zack, who was trying to stay awake but whose heavy-lidded eyes told a different story. She slid a little farther over on her bed. "Zack, can you come lie here for a bit?" she asked softly, just needing the touch, the warmth. He didn't hesitate, just stood up and carefully slid onto the bed next to her, pulling her close for a hug. She curled into him.

"I love you," he said softly, dropping a small kiss on the top of her head. She sighed gently. The love she felt for Zack was so different from the lust she had felt for Ryan. It felt almost grown-up, settled, important.

"I love you too," she responded quietly, feeling a sense of calm contentment wash over her as he pulled her impossibly closer. He was strong and sure and held her like she was the most precious thing in his life.

"Ali, this may not be the right time..." He paused,

shifting his hold of her and then carding his hand through her long hair. "I wanted flowers and champagne. But we're a family now, and I love both of you so much."

Allison snuggled closer, burying her face in his neck, inhaling the familiar scent of him and smiled a secret smile he would never see. She knew what he was going to say.

"Allison, will you marry me?" It really was the easiest question she had ever been asked.

"Yes, Zack I will. I'll marry you"

* * * *

Ryan refused the pain meds that Nathan held out, still in a daze at what his mom had said when Nathan had handed him the phone. She was over the moon, delighted, and she'd congratulated him and Allison, and wanted to know everything.

Most important of all though, she said she understood, said she had spoken to Allison a few times and knew Ryan had fallen in love with someone else, knew that person was Nathan. She told him off like he was a small child for the ex-sex he'd been having. Ryan blushed at that, but then she added something along the lines of 'I'm a gran again. Oh, Ryan, I'm so proud."

The meds made him sleepy, and he didn't want sleepy and disoriented. He wanted real. He wanted to try and kiss Nathan, hug Nathan, sleep with Nathan, and he needed to feel tonight, really feel.

Somehow Nathan had managed to help him shower, covering his neck, washing his hair. He'd left Ryan sitting on the edge of the bed wrapped in a towel, promising he would be back soon.

When he returned, he was laden down with spicy smelling hot pizza and Wal-Mart bags that revealed new jeans, clean t-shirts, sweatshirts, and heavens, new boxers. It was like Christmas. Nathan grabbed the quickest shower in history, foregoing a shave, and then both dressed in the new T's and boxers. They sat cross-legged opposite each other on the bed, eating pizza, Ryan struggling a bit but managing to eat some of it nonetheless.

When he finished, Nathan placed the box on the floor next to the bed and returned to his favorite pastime; staring at Ryan. Ryan, for his part, decided he needed to touch, needed to feel, and he ran hands over broad shoulders and against hot skin, learning Nathan's body, cupping his face and leaning in to touch lips. They couldn't do much more. Nathan still struggled to breathe with his broken ribs, but Ryan was content to touch, to be touched. Soft breathing was exchanged, with eyes closed and fingers seeking anchors in soft t-shirt material.

"Love you," Nathan whispered against Ryan's lips, more vibration than words. Ryan caught the words close to him, savored the feel of them, and craved their warmth.

"I love you too." He traced Nathan's lips with the tip of his tongue, darting in for a quick taste before retreating to lie back on the bed, encouraging Nathan to lie as close as was comfortable, pulling covers over them and switching off the light. Ryan curled into his Nathan, his arms wrapped round him and sleep claimed them both before they even had time for conscious thought.

* * * *

Ryan woke in the night, unable to move from the pain, and must have made a noise because Nathan was instantly awake and right there with water and tablets. He helped Ryan to lie on his stomach, when before he had been lying on his side, and Ryan sighed in thanks. Some of the tension knotting in him started to dissipate. He turned his head to face Nathan, knowing this was a conversation he needed to have.

"Some of these marks on your back may scar," Nathan started softly. "I am so sorry."

"No…'pology," Ryan muttered.

"I should never have run. If I'd stayed in New York then none of this would have happened," Nathan pointed out, sorrow filling his voice, his hands twisted in his short hair, a kind of raw despair on his face. Ryan pushed through the pain, lifting a hand to capture one of Nathan's, easing it down to hold it as tight as he could.

"Made…you…run." He pushed the words out, pronouncing each as clearly as he could. Tears formed in his eyes from a combination of pain and distress at what he was saying; Nathan could have died on that mountain, the same way that David Jackson had, trapped in the burning and twisted metal. It didn't bear thinking about. The thought of losing Nathan, of losing him to the fire, his body… It was too much to even think about, let alone articulate.

"Ryan, you need to sleep. Shut your eyes."

Ryan closed his eyes, his hand still loose in Nathan's, and he let Nathan's voice wash over him as the painkillers started their work on his tortured muscles and stretched tight, hot skin.

* * * *

Nathan carried on a one-sided conversation, willing Ryan to relax and let sleep take him to a place where he could begin to heal. "Do you remember when we first met, when I had that first call back, and it was just us, you and your camera and I was alternating between being pissed I had lost the last job and overwhelmed that I had gotten to work with you?"

He waited for Ryan to nod, a sleepy smile loosening his tight pain-thinned lips before continuing.

"You walked in; I had Googled you, checked out your portfolio, and you were nothing like what I was expecting. I mean, the gossip columns said you were tall, but when I stood up and you were still like towering over me, I felt so small. Then to add insult to injury, your hands, dude, so big and warm. When we shook hands, you won't believe what went through my head. Do you know there and then I knew I was screwed, I mean I had to do the whole model thing, and I was crushing so hard on the straight guy with the girlfriend. So yeah, screwed."

Nathan looked down at Ryan's face, his features relaxed in sleep, his breathing even and shallow. "Worst of all though, Ryan, it wasn't lust. It wasn't really crushing. It was like I knew you were the other half of me, and I just had to wait for you to see that I was the other half of you."

* * * *

The plane touched down at one in the afternoon the following day, spitting out Ortizes and Richardsons like no tomorrow. It had taken some doing, but if the boys weren't able to get to them, then they sure as hell were going to go to the boys. They organized hotel rooms, and then the Ortiz group maneuvered, like an entire army, to the hospital, sat in the maternity waiting room and waited. No one contacted either man; no one hassled anyone to see Allison. They just waited, knowing sooner or later someone would spot them.

"Are you... the nurse at the desk said you... are you related to Ryan?"

Jeff stood, held out his hand. "I'm Jeff, Ryan's brother. This is my wife, and mom, dad, and Kathy, my, our, sister." It was an overwhelming list of people to introduce, and the other man blinked at the overload of information.

"I'm Zack, er, Allison's partner."

* * * *

Zack shook Jeff's hand, craning to look up at him, on the tip of his tongue to comment on his height. He went round meeting his daughter's father's family, trying to recall names, remember faces. "Ryan is coming down in a while. He and Nathan are holed up nearby. He's not in a good way."

"I know, emergency tracheotomy, extensive damage to his back, Nathan said." Jeff catalogued the injuries in such a matter-of-fact way that Zack was taken aback until Kathy snarked something about him being a surgeon and having a cold heart, getting a punch on the arm from Jeff as an immediate comeback.

"Okay, well, I mean, do you wanna come through and see Allison?"

"I'll go." This came from Ryan's mom. Maggie? "It'll be too much for all of us to go in. I'll see Allison, and y'all go see the baby, see Millie."

"But, Mom, surely you want to—"

"I want to see Allison first, Kathy, then I'll come down, I promise."

* * * *

Nathan had to help Ryan dress entirely, his muscles kept spasming, and pain was etched on his face. Nathan handed him the water and meds, which Ryan downed immediately with a grateful smile.

Nathan had talked a bit about going back to New York when Ryan felt up to it. Ryan had nodded his agreement, but inside Nathan thought it was going to be impossible to tear Ryan away from Millie, and Nathan knew with quiet certainty that for the foreseeable future, where Ryan was, Nathan would be. No, not even just for the near future, but on a much more permanent basis.

It was Nathan who saw them all leaning in a row against the NICU window, talking gently and, every so often, pointing in at, he assumed, Millie. A group of Ortiz and Richardson family members.

"Ryan, looks like we have company."

* * * *

Day twelve was a milestone. The heavy bandages and stitches that had been applied in the field needed removing, and Nathan knew Ryan was apprehensive. His family, and Nathan's for that matter, had left a few days before, none the wiser that Ryan was scared to death wondering what the doctor would find on his back. Jeff had tried to look, but Ryan just faced him steadily and refused to let him touch it. Jeff had bitched, but Ryan was not going to back down. He hadn't let anyone touch his back, or his throat, and Nathan was struggling to understand why.

"Because I'm pretty," Ryan blurted out suddenly, his throat infinitely better. At least he was talking, not quite at full Ryan level, but slowly getting there. This odd response was a result of Nathan's insistence on wanting to be in the room when they assessed the injuries. It wasn't the first time Nathan had pushed, and if he didn't get his way, it wouldn't be the last, but those three words were so at odds with what he thought Ryan may say it stunned Nathan into premature silence.

"Okay, I'm shallow," Ryan continued. "I know it's stupid, but people say I have a nice back, soft, smooth, strong, and I was kinda proud of it." His breathing hitched, and Nathan knew the signs of an oncoming Ortiz breakdown.

"Proud of your back?" Nathan tried not to sound incredulous, but he must have sounded just tha way because the response he got from Ryan was instant and messy. Ryan slumped down onto the bed.

"I don't really mean that; I don't know what I mean. I just don't know."

Nathan fell to his knees in front of Ryan, peering up at his him through his hair. "It's not shallow to worry about what you look like, Ryan. Jeez, my whole career kinda depends on it at the moment."

"I'm not…" Ryan swallowed, his eyes still leaking, his hands twisted in the covers on either side of him, "Jesus, fuck, Nathan, I don't give a shit about… what I look like… I don't know what I mean."

"Ryan, you're not making any sense."

"Like I don't know that. This is all screwed to hell. Ignore me, I'm just…will you stay with me?" Ryan stared straight into Nathan's eyes, the green and brown in his hazel eyes sparkling with unshed tears.

"Of course I will, Ryan, you know I'll go in with you, hold your hand," Nathan reassured gently.

"I-I didn't mean that, not really, I meant, even if I am scarred and shit, will you stay with me?"

Nathan sat back on his heels, feeling as if a huge weight had just knocked him sideways. This was what was upsetting Ryan? The thought that Nathan couldn't love a less than physically perfect body? Nathan's first reaction was anger. Did Ryan really think he was that shallow? His next reaction was that Ryan's head wasn't right. They had literally been to hell and back. No wonder he was screwed.

Then it kind of hit him all at once. Ryan had hinted several times that Nathan didn't have to stay with him, didn't have to become an instant stepdad to a child that was Ryan's ex's, that it was okay if he felt it was all too much. This latest outburst was just another way of giving Nathan an out, and it was the last time that this was being brought up if Nathan had anything to do with it.

"When you found me in the apartment, Ryan, when I was pinned down by my legs under that steel, what if I'd been paralyzed when you pulled me out?"

"Fuck, Nathan."

"Seriously. We somehow managed to get down the

mountain and got to help, but what if I couldn't have walked, what if I could never walk again? What would you do?"

"Do?"

"Would you leave me?"

"Dude."

"And then what if an ex of mine revealed she was having my baby? Would you try and understand why it all happened or would you have run screaming for the hills?"

Ryan looked shocked. "Shit, I wouldn't do that, you know I wouldn't," he said.

"So, time to get you to the hospital and get you sorted, pretty boy, yeah?"

CHAPTER 18

The doctor took some details, simple stuff, nothing too heavy. Questions that even Nathan could answer. He strayed into some heavier questions, made some brief suggestions about therapy, both physical and psychological, and Nathan sensed Ryan tensing next to him. He filed the reaction away for further thought.

Then it was time. Time for the doctor to start peeling away the dressings. He called in a nurse, donned gloves, pulled a tray closer and gently reassured Ryan. Nathan pulled a chair over to sit next to Ryan's head, and the doctor began, keeping up a running dialogue of what he was doing. "...difficult to see through some of the swelling... If we cut this away... Can I have some local here? ... Looking good... What we have here are some very healthy looking wounds, Mr Ortiz... did a good job. You may have a scar there, nothing plastic surgery won't fix..."

"I won't be doing that. If it scars, it scars," Ryan said, wincing at the pain and smiling at the same time.

"What about your pretty back?" Nathan smirked, reaching over and touching Ryan's hand softly.

"Are you ever gonna forget I said that?"

"Never."

"Bastard."

"Yep, but you know you love me."

"Yeah, I do."

EPILOGUE

The magazine did a ten-page spread on the journey that their photographer had taken. It focused on the human story, the minute details of their quest with Laurie and Jason, the timely intervention of the dog, Oscar, and the individual stories of the heroes that had helped Ryan Ortiz and his boyfriend, Nathan Richardson, survive that awful day.

It spoke of the two men living their lives, of the hope that emerged from a destroyed LA, and it counted the number of people that had lost their lives.

Millie was a happy, healthy child, and Zack and Allison were never blessed with other children. Millie was their life, and she was Ryan's true child— tall, strong, beautiful and funny. She married when she was twenty-six and had three children that Grandpas Nathan and Ryan spoiled rotten. She was very close to both her real dad and to Zack, winding them equally 'round her little finger, much to her mom's despair.

Laurie went on to Yale and kept Ryan and Nathan informed of her every step in the form of emails that arrived as regular as clockwork every month. They replied to every one, well, Ryan did, but Nathan always added a few sentences as a postscript. They formed the basis of a series of books she wrote and dedicated to the men that saved her.

Jason was the founder of the Children's Disaster Center Program, present at every major disaster in the US helping children cope and survive, reuniting children with parents, and bringing back hope to the families torn apart by nature.

And Nathan and Ryan?

Their "goodbye, we're leaving the limelight" spread in *Style* was the biggest selling cover story ever, not least in part due to the stories surrounding the two men and their battle to escape LA.

They stayed in Phoenix, Ryan starting a photography studio, Nathan commuting to new television studios spread throughout the country when he needed to, acting, living, and loving until they told everyone that the call of wanting to be close to their parents and extended family made them move to Kentucky, equidistant between both families. Nathan knew why they really moved. Millie had turned four and was torn between Papa Ryan and her daddy Zack. It wasn't right in Ryan's mind to do this to her, and despite arguments, he finally persuaded Nathan to go home.

When they got to Kentucky, they bought land, built a house with enough room for dogs and horses, and they loved there until the day that cancer meant Nathan had to leave. He was seventy-four. He wanted to be buried on their land so he could remain close to Ryan even in death. Ryan was there alone for only a year, his own death one that could only be put down to loneliness. He had family, and he was a grandfather, a father, and a brother, but at the end of the day, without Nathan, he felt like he was nothing at all.

When they buried Ryan in the same place as Nathan, Millie erected a simple headstone. It had their names, one date —May 2011— and just a simple set of words.

Through fire they saved each other.

The End

THE AFTERMATH OF THE 2011 QUAKE

As for the city of dreams, in LA there were seven thousand three hundred and forty-nine confirmed deaths in the great quake of 2011. Many more people were declared missing, bringing the suspected death toll nearer nine thousand. The powers that be decided never to rebuild downtown LA, never to sit so many human lives on such a delicate, imbalanced earth. By 2014 the area had become an area of transients, the homeless, the destitute, and slowly but surely, old Los Angeles started to disappear.

The government tried to step in, but the very idea of one place to go, one place where it didn't matter who you were or what you had done made it a no-go area for regeneration. People who had lived there and loved there had lost everything. Businesses failed, smaller companies went bankrupt, and all that was good seemed to leave.

By 2020 the area was under martial law, the old Hollywood, downtown LA, and the beaches lost in a quagmire of red tape and suspicion; eventually the land was bought up by a government-backed conglomerate who promised cleanup. They fought hard, started rebuilding, started encouraging business, and by 2022, the area had started its infant regeneration. In 2023, a small, almost-nothing earthquake sent people scurrying from New Los

Angeles.

No one really ever returned, and the land slowly became reclaimed by desert and forest, finally designated a national park in 2052.

ALSO BY R J SCOTT

Available at **Silver Publishing**:

Oracle
Moments
The Christmas Throwaway
The Heart of Texas
Valentine 2525
All the King's Men
Back Home (April 2011)

THE FIRE TRILOGY
Kian

THE FITZWARREN INHERITANCE
The Psychic's Tale, by Chris Quinton
The Soldier's Tale, by RJ Scott
The Searcher's Tale, by Sue Brown

Available at **Dreamspinner Press**:

Two Plus One
"Ascension" in *A Brush of Wings*

AWARDS:

Best Paranormal Author 2010
Love Romance Café
Nomination

Best GBLTQ Author 2010
Love Romance Café
Nomination

Oracle
Best Gay Paranormal / Horror 2010
Elisa Rolle's Rainbow Awards
Honorable Mention (5th)

Oracle
Best Cover 2010
Love Romance Café
Nomination

CPSIA information can be obtained at www.ICGtesting.com
Printed in the USA
LVOW130123281112

309058LV00003B/792/P